Here's How You Fly
A Novel
Michael Anthony Adams, Jr.

SIX SEEDS PRESS
Baltimore, MD

First Edition
Copyright © 2025 Michael Anthony
Adams, Jr.

Originally published in paperback by Six Seeds Press
Baltimore, MD
October 2025

ISBN: 978-1-952240-34-8

All rights reserved.

The story presented here is a work of fiction. Names, characters, places, and incidents are the product of the author's imagination or are used fictitiously. Any resemblance to actual persons, living or dead, events or locales is entirely coincidental.

Cover Design © 2025 PJ Adams
Portrait of Michael Anthony Adams, Jr.
© 2014 PJ Adams

Also by Michael Anthony Adams, Jr. and Published by Six Seeds Press

Novels:
The Adversary's Good News
Crossroads Blues

Short Stories:
Spare Change
Psychedelicizations
The American Apocalypse
The Cars Behind, Beside Us
Welcome to the Modern World, Charlie
Notes from the Idle Mind

Memoir:
Disorder

Poetry:
We Are the Underground
From Now to You
Recipe for a Future Theogony
Indigo Glow
The Tree Outside My Window
At the Side of the Road
Soundtrack for the New Millennium

Young Adult:
Here's How You Fly

www.MichaelAnthonyAdamsJr.com

HERE'S HOW YOU FLY
for my children

HERE'S HOW YOU FLY

Content Warning
(Please Read)

This book depicts teenagers grappling with serious issues, including drug and alcohol abuse, sexual assault, underage pregnancy, homophobia, and racism. If you are not comfortable with your child confronting these issues on their own, I urge you to read this book with them.

I.

1.

Like the sounds hidden in a record's grooves, smoke hung heavy and thick. It obscured the light from above as if the smog from his California childhood had followed him across the country. His dad still lived there, in Southern California. He'd been in Virginia for three years, since the summer of 1988. Now it was 1991. Not that the year made any difference. He was in ninth grade. Childhood—along with the Pacific Ocean breeze—was a distant dream.

He took a drag off his cigarette, exhaled, and added another layer to the smoke already choking them in that packed room. They were in the church's outbuilding. The smoke's scent was buried deep in the cheap carpet. Its remnants discolored the walls. He said, "My name is Josh, and I guess I'm an alcoholic."

Beneath the haze, the room remained quiet and still. The scattered adults who had raised their hands to share dropped them back into their laps. All the eyes—young and old—turned to Josh. He looked down to avoid their gazes, even that of the girl in the corner who was about his age. She reminded him of his friend, Melody Fisher. Like Melody, she was thin, in a short jean skirt, rainbow tights, and a black tee shirt. Her stringy blond hair lay limp across her shoulders. Melody's hair was curly. Josh didn't know the girl in the corner. He didn't know any of these people.

"I'm sure you all remember what happened the last time I came here," Josh said. "Well, this past weekend was no different."

That past weekend, Josh had told his mom he was spending the night with Todd Campbell. Todd had told his mom he was spending the night at Josh's. They both wound up sleeping alone, one of them in the cab of a truck and the other in the backseat of a car, in Melody's father's backyard. The night had grown too cold to sleep in the woods across from Carrie's, Josh's girlfriend's, place. But in only their leather jackets, the night wasn't much warmer in those broken down automobiles. Melody woke them before 5:00 am, before her father looked out the kitchen window and spotted them there. Her breath made a mist in the chilly morning air.

She said, "You look defiant even in your sleep, Josh." He'd been sleeping on his back with his head tilted back and his hands clasped in his lap.

Josh and Todd each dropped a hit of acid they'd purchased the night before, and they walked down the road to figure out where they might find some breakfast. But they were broke. Every dime they'd scrounged together had gone to buy the drugs they were on, the liquor they drank the night before, and the beer in the duffel bag Todd was carrying. A local biker gang ran an acid lab one more county south of the city of Richmond from where Todd and Josh were in Potterfield County. All the kids—the metalheads, the skaters, and the deadheads—had been eating acid regularly for almost a year by then. Josh and Todd were no different.

Todd's uncle was a member of that biker gang. Todd had grown up down on Route One, Jeff Davis Highway, the Petersburg Pike, across from the Stonewall Park housing projects. He and his mom had moved to Josh's town, the town of Louthain, only a year before. They were fleeing Todd's abusive father.

When Josh saw Todd walking through their middle school hallway on the first day of eighth grade, he knew they had to be friends. Todd was wearing a tee shirt for the thrash metal band Megadeth and a black leather jacket with tassels dangling off its sleeves. The tee shirt had the band's logo printed over a skull with its mouth clamped shut and metal blinders over its eyes and ears. When Josh later discovered Todd played the guitar, he introduced himself in the lunchroom. "I want to start a band," he said.

Todd was a year older than Josh. He'd been held back in fifth grade. His hair was longer than Josh's too, which dangled in front of Josh's eyes in the front and came down to the base of his neck in the back. Todd would make the perfect lead guitarist for Josh's imaginary band. They became friends. They exchanged song lyrics and guitar riffs. They huffed freon out of Josh's parents' air conditioner.

"I'm going to turn you into the thief I should have become," Todd said to Josh one day. They'd just stolen a pack of cigarettes from the local 7-11. Todd had bumped into the counter and knocked a pack of generic smokes back into the arcade room where Josh was already waiting. Josh pocketed the cigarettes, and they left separately.

Josh liked Todd's plan about teaching him to become a thief. It might help him get back to California, but not to his dad's place in Orange County. Josh wanted to run away to Hollywood when he turned 16. Todd agreed to go with him. Josh had a knack for drawing people into his fantasies. None of those ideas kept Josh from making out with Todd's girlfriend though when Todd got locked up at the end of the school year for breaking probation.

Todd's girlfriend, Tina, wasn't allowed to have boys in her room, but that never kept Todd out of there. And she still took a long walk with Josh while Todd was locked up. The two of them weaved through back streets and trails to a wide open field. They couldn't see the road in any direction. The grass grew tall all around them. It swayed beneath the springtime breeze.

"Are you ready?" Tina asked. Josh nodded. The sky was as blue as the ocean Josh remembered from Southern California. The clouds were blots on the endless expanse. Josh made up meanings for their various contortions.

Tina and Josh had already known one another for a couple years. They'd dated briefly in seventh grade, before Josh had even met Todd, but they'd never been as close as they were that afternoon. And they never were again. Both of them kept their mouths shut about it. Todd never found out.

Before Todd got out of the detention center, Josh started dating Carrie Condrey. Carrie was a year younger than Josh. But with her hair hanging almost to her waist, she'd matured early. And when Carrie revealed to Josh what her 17-year-old brother had already done to her, Josh was shaken.

"I've never told anybody about that before," Carrie said.

Josh sat still in his chair in his mother's den, his mouth agape, the telephone in his hand, the receiver to his ear.

"Are you okay?" Carrie asked.

The night outside the window to Josh's right was black. He said, "Yeah. I guess I am."

"Do you hate me?"

Josh's face contorted. "No, I don't hate you. I hate your brother," he said. He couldn't understand how one person could visit that kind of suffering upon another person. It opened up a brand new wound in Josh's mind.

That summer, Josh lost his virginity to Carrie beside the television on the carpet upstairs in Josh's home. The TV set was tuned into some cartoon, but neither of them were paying attention. Josh's mother was downstairs cooking dinner. His stepdad was still at work.

That past weekend, Josh had convinced Carrie to let Tina sleep over at her place. Carrie and Tina weren't friends. They weren't enemies though either. Carrie agreed for Josh's sake. He and Todd would sleep in the woods across the street. They could sneak in through Carrie's bedroom window and visit the two girls in the middle of the night. It made Josh feel like he was in some old, youth rebellion movie from the 1970s, the kind of movie he would have watched on the floor of his mother's den after his father first left them alone.

The four teenagers spent the afternoon listening to thrash metal albums Josh had copied Carrie from his own tapes and CDs on a boombox in the shed in Carrie's backyard. That shed was where Carrie and Josh had often retreated during the summer. It was hot and sticky. It smelled of sweat, but it was the one place neither her older brothers nor her mother would discover them.

That afternoon, the four of them were all in there, smoking cigarettes and drinking a bottle of cheap wine. That evening, they all went to the mall together. That's where Josh and Todd each bought a hit of acid. Then the four of them walked over to Dave's, a pool hall across the street. Carrie and Tina convinced an older man to buy them a bottle of Everclear—190 proof grain alcohol— and a case of beer.

They drank the bottle that night. Carrie and Tina mixed it with soda. Josh and Todd drank it straight. As if ripping the flesh from their esophaguses, the Everclear burned their throats. With every sip, they closed their eyes and shook their heads. They put the acid—folded up in a little strip of paper—into a pack of cigarettes, which they forgot about until the next day. The remnants of that case of beer was what Todd was carrying in a duffel bag when he and Josh left Melody's backyard the following morning.

"When we snuck in through my girlfriend's window, we were already drunk." Josh wasn't looking at anybody in the meeting as he spoke, not the blond girl in the corner, not the preppy guy in a Polo shirt across from him, not even the tall gangly kid, sitting next to the preppy kid and smiling at Josh like he could relate. "We made too much noise and woke her mom up. Todd and I had to hide in the closet. When she came in, Carrie's mom started screaming at her. As soon as her mom went back to bed, Carrie said we had to go. She was going to get in trouble.

"We went back out the window, and we were just wandering around the neighborhood, drinking beers, when this cop shined his light on us. The cop said something, but we didn't listen. We took off running. We ditched the beer somewhere in the woods. We figured we could dig it back up once we were safe—"

A gruff voice broke into Josh's monologue. "That's enough," some gray-haired old man said. "If we want to learn how to get drunk, we'll call on you."

Josh sat still. He narrowed his eyes. His cheeks burned red. His hands started trembling.

Everybody was staring at him. He'd had enough. He didn't want to be there. He didn't care if his mom wanted him to go to that AA meeting. He didn't care if he wound up in a psych ward that night.

He stood up. He grabbed his leather motorcycle jacket off the back of his chair. The snaps and buckles on it jingled and jangled. Everybody—the gray-haired old man, the blond girl, the preppy guy, the gangly kid, and the rest—stared at him. Josh grabbed his cigarettes and his Harley-Davidson zippo lighter off the floor. He stormed out the meeting into the night.

2.

As the cool November air broke on Josh's face, he inhaled. The distant scent of neighborhood chimneys exuded smoke. In the darkness, the church across the parking lot was a harpooned whale. A graveyard—the speared whale's intestines—spilled out beside it.

"You've got your warrior back," Josh whispered to the devil who he believed could hear him through the night air.

He zipped up his jacket and lit another cigarette. Carrie's neighborhood wasn't far from there. Josh thought about sneaking off to go visit her, but he had to wait for his mom to pick him up. Despite his bravado, he still didn't want to wind up in a psych ward that same night. That's where his mom and Dr. Meyer, his psychologist, had been threatening to send him if things didn't turn around. "This sucks," Josh said, and he wandered off to the graveyard. That was a fitting place for a Satanist to wait, he figured.

He was standing in the middle of the graveyard, trying to read the faded tombstones in the dark, and puffing off his smoke when a voice behind him intruded on his thoughts. "Hey, man," the voice said.

Josh turned around. For a second, he thought the devil might have materialized in response to his call. But it wasn't a spirit. It was a corporeal form.

It was the preppy kid in the Polo shirt from the meeting. Like Josh, he was thin and wiry, but significantly shorter. His complexion appeared healthy. He had a slight tan even in the fall. The tips of his tightly cropped, curly hair were bleached blond, and his khakis were much baggier than Josh's skintight jeans. "What do you want?" Josh asked.

"Just to talk," the preppy kid said. "I'm Matt."

Josh nodded. He didn't introduce himself in return, and he didn't shake Matt's hand when he extended it. Matt stood awkwardly for a moment. His hand hung like a dead branch in the wind before he dropped it back to his side again. He pulled out his own cigarette. The preppy kid smoked Camels. *Figures*, Josh thought. Josh smoked Marlboro Reds. "You got a light?" Matt asked.

Josh nodded. He walked over to Matt. He lit his cigarette for him with the Harley-Davidson zippo he'd so carefully made sure to retrieve from the floor. It burned as bright as the bush Moses had witnessed in the desert. Josh had turned the flame on the lighter way up like the lighter Kenickie had used in the movie *Grease*, which Josh had loved so much as a kid. It had only been a year since Josh had last imagined himself as Danny Zuko, that film's main character. The lighter had been a gift from Melody that past summer. She'd stolen it from a store at the mall. She'd given it to Josh because he was her best friend.

Matt took a long drag off his cigarette. He exhaled an amorphous cloud like the Rorschach blots Josh had seen in the sky in the field that afternoon with Tina, but this time he couldn't create shapes out of it.

"Nice lighter," Matt said.

Josh nodded. "My friend gave it to me," he said.

Melody and Josh had been friends since Josh had started seventh grade. Back then Melody was breaking up with Eric Graham, a boy who rode Josh's bus. Eric and Melody were both a year ahead of Josh. Eric wore a Led Zeppelin patch on the back of his acid-washed jean jacket. He and Josh talked about music sometimes. He was the first person who ever smoked Josh up on marijuana at the end of sixth grade. They were down off a path through the woods near Eric's bus stop. Josh heaved and coughed. "Smoke much?" Eric asked. Josh glared at him.

Eric was also the first lead guitarist for Josh's imaginary band. Although, he never knew that. That fact only existed in Josh's imagination.

"If you want to sing, you need to take vocal lessons," Eric told Josh one day when they were smoking pot on that same trail through the woods where Josh had first smoked marijuana.

"Jimi Hendrix never took guitar lessons," Josh said. Eric shrugged. He didn't know if that was true, and he didn't know what it had to do with Josh becoming a singer.

Melody asked Josh to give her his phone number while he was sniffing a bottle of glue out on the bus loop at school. Josh didn't know if the glue actually got him high. It made him feel a little light-headed, but that could have been an influx of oxygen from the depth of his own breathing as well. He didn't know much about drugs yet. He'd merely been inspired by the Ramones' song, *Now I Wanna Sniff Some Glue*. He wanted the kids at school to see him sniffing that glue though. Then they might have some idea what he was going through.

He gave Melody his number because he thought she

was pretty. But Melody started calling Josh to find out things about Eric. Josh was okay with that. He had crushes on other girls. Some of them Melody already knew, and she promised to introduce him to them.

Before the two of them knew it, Josh and Melody were talking on the phone after school every day. Soon Melody started calling Josh her best friend. That got him in good with all the metalheads a year ahead of him. He started dating the girls in Melody's grade who he had crushes on. All his friends wound up being from her neighborhood. That made him even more intimidating than he already was to the rich kids from his own neighborhood in his own grade. Melody cried when she said goodbye to Josh at the end of her eighth grade year. They were going to wind up at different high schools. Her last day of eighth grade should have been goodbye forever.

But Melody didn't start high school the following year. That summer, she skipped out on summer school. She got held back. Her parents split up. She moved with her mom into the same apartment complex in Josh's district that Todd moved into. She only spent every other weekend at her dad's place in her old neighborhood. She and Josh would wind up at the same high school, and she and Josh wound up in the same grade.

The faculty at their middle school thought Melody and Josh were boyfriend and girlfriend. They were so close. They were inseparable. But the truth was Melody only dated boys in high school, boys who picked her up at the end of the middle school day in cars. She'd dash out to the parking lot and hop in with whatever boy was interested in her at the moment. She was supposed to be in high school herself after all. It made for complicated feelings between Josh and Melody, but they agreed they should never date unless they ran away to Hollywood together.

Then maybe…

Josh and Melody sang duets of glam metal songs over the phone. From different neighborhoods across the county from one another, they counted to three and pressed play on their tapes at the exact same time. Josh screeched the first lines of a song over the phone. His voice cracked. He could barely reach the notes. Even though the man who sang them was almost as old as his mom.

Melody cried the next lines back to him. She was closer to the right pitch, but without any training, she overshot it.

They sang the chorus in unison. They thought they sounded like rock stars. Someday when they were both famous, they'd sing that duet together on a stage in front of thousands of adoring fans. They'd explain to music magazines like the ones Josh stole out of local drug stores how they'd started singing that song together when they were still kids in middle school in a county on the outskirts of Richmond, VA long before they showed up in Los Angeles.

Josh and Melody went to see AC/DC, Aerosmith, and Mötley Crüe together. Unlike the concerts Josh had been to before he'd met Melody, he hardly remembered any of those shows. Melody scored so much weed for them from the high school boys flirting with her. She showed up at the Richmond Coliseum in her short skirt and tee shirt tied off at the waist to reveal her midriff. At every whiff of pot, she smiled and introduced Josh as her cousin. By the time the main acts came on, Josh was strolling through an ethereal plane.

Melody even spent the night at Josh's place after those concerts. They were such good friends. Their parents allowed it even though Melody's dad had reservations.

Melody was supposed to sleep in the guest room, but the two of them often wound up sharing cigarettes all night in Josh's twin bed. Nothing ever happened between them though. One night while they were lying in bed, Melody told Josh his stepdad was a creep. He was always checking her out. He was almost 40 years old.

"He checks everyone out," Josh said. He was drifting off to sleep. "That's why he'll take us to concerts. He wants to look at the girls."

Melody nodded in the darkness. "I'll bet he smokes pot," she said, staring at the ceiling.

"I know he smokes pot," Josh said. "I've pinched his bag."

Once Josh knew the scent of marijuana, he was certain he'd smelt it in his parents' bedroom on weekend mornings. One evening when his mom and stepdad were out, Josh scoured the room to find their bag.

On the corner of a shelf at the top of his stepdad's closet, behind a box of pornographic videos and magazines, a blue duffel bag appeared. In it, there was a small pipe, some papers, and a couple ounces of marijuana in a large Ziplock baggie. Once he found it, Josh started taking little pinches out of it every now and then. Even if Bill did discover some of his pot was missing, he couldn't ask Josh about it. He couldn't reveal to the boy he had what Josh's mom said he should never do. Bill would have to imagine he'd smoked more than he thought.

Matt asked, "So did you ever find that beer you ditched?"

Josh smiled. "Yeah, man," he said, "once we lost that cop, we circled around to get back to where we dumped it."

"That's good," Matt said. "I know I would have freaked out if I lost a whole case of beer."

"You still drink?" Josh asked. He was almost salivating at the thought of cracking one open with the preppy kid right then. Matt might have even had a six pack stashed in the old, dingy white Ford Escort he always showed up in.

"No, man. I got sober two years ago."

"Oh," Josh said. "Why did you do that?"

"I got sick and tired of being sick and tired."

"What's that supposed to mean?" Josh asked.

"It means drinking and drugs weren't for me anymore," Matt said to Josh after another drag off his cigarette. "If they ever really were," he added.

Josh tilted his head to the side. He narrowed his eyes. On some level, he already knew what Matt was talking about.

Drinking and drugs had never been fun for him. It was something he did out of necessity as if he were a machine whose crank had been wound through his childhood. During his middle school years, he'd simply acted as his programming had dictated. He didn't have free will. Heavy drinking and drug abuse had been predetermined for him. Whether it was the coils of his DNA unraveling or his spirit's destiny being revealed, Josh hadn't started drinking and doing drugs to have fun. For some reason he never understood, he had always done both only because he had to. "I think I know what you mean," he said.

Josh's words were barely audible, but Matt perked up. He realized what he'd said had reached through the metalhead's fog and touched his heart. Old timers in AA had told Matt that could happen, but the truth had never been so apparently manifest to him. Wanting to keep Josh engaged, he asked, "So did you get a chance to drink those beers?"

"No. They're in my girlfriend's shed now. We'll drink them next chance we get though."

"You don't have to do that, you know," Matt said.

Josh creased his eyes even deeper. He peered through the night as if there were shapes in the darkness only he could make out. "No, I think I do," he said. "Even if I don't want to, I think I do."

Matt nodded. He understood what Josh was saying. He asked, "You ate that acid though, right?"

3.

After they'd eaten the acid, Josh and Todd walked circles around Melody's cold neighborhood. There was frost on the ground. The two boys' teeth chattered. They rubbed their hands together to try generating some warmth. The sun came out. That brought a miniscule amount of heat to the world. It shone through the leaves overhead to shed pockets of shadows across the road's concrete. When they couldn't take the cold and hunger any longer, Josh and Todd made their way back to Carrie's.

It wasn't even 8:30 in the morning when the two hungry, disheveled metalheads wound up there. They ditched the beer in the shed in the backyard, and they rang the doorbell.

When she answered, Carrie's mom looked at them askance, but she summoned her daughter and Tina anyway.

In her pajamas, Carrie made the boys breakfast—toast with jelly. Under the influence of LSD, the purple toast with the white swirls of butter looked like a tie-dyed tee shirt. It was simultaneously psychedelic and stomach churning, but Josh and Todd ate it anyway. While the girls got dressed, the boys settled down in the living room to watch television with Carrie's mom.

Star Trek came on. Captain Kirk was fighting a giant, green reptile. It had to be some sort of alien. The episode was confusing. Everybody kept dying and coming back to life.

"When Scotty beams them up, did you ever notice how a little piece of them—that light right in the center of their chests—takes longer to disappear than the rest?" Josh asked nobody. "That's their soul," he said. He grinned.

Todd didn't budge. Carrie's mom tilted her head to the side. She looked at the two boys out of the corner of her eye. Josh noticed that. He knew she knew they were on drugs. Josh's palms started sweating. He rubbed them down his jeans' legs. He wanted to get out of her house.

At the next commercial break, when Carrie's mom went to use the bathroom, Josh leaned over to Todd. He said, "Hey man, we've got to get out of here. She knows." He jerked his thumb back to point toward the corner around which Carrie's mom had disappeared. He hoped he was whispering.

Todd's eyes opened wide. His jaw dropped. The two boys hopped up from their seats—Josh on the couch, Todd slouched in a chair—as if the room were on fire. They grabbed their leather jackets off the kitchen table, and they ran out of the house. They didn't even say goodbye to Carrie or Tina.

The two girls heard the screen door slam from where they were still getting ready in Carrie's bedroom. They looked at one another. Carrie was angry the boys had come to her home in their state. If her mom knew what they were doing, she would be in real trouble. She intended to have a serious talk with Josh that night, once his trip was over. But she never got the chance. Too much happened before Josh made it home. The weekend had been a potential disaster. If her mom had any idea what had happened that day and the night before, Carrie might never be allowed to see Josh again. In fact, she would probably be grounded for months, and that meant she'd be able to do a lot less than see Josh.

Once they were outside in the neighborhood, Josh and Todd laughed at their panic. The sun shone down on them. Things couldn't have been as dire as they'd imagined. They decided they should head back over to Melody's. The day had warmed some. The air felt as fresh as the exhaust from a washing machine. The sky was crisp and blue. Even the dead leaves on the trees swayed like there was life after death. Josh and Todd talked and laughed all the way over to Melody's place. They forgot about what they were afraid Carrie's mom might know. They even forgot they were tripping. Everything seemed so normal. That feeling was simply how they lived their lives now.

Melody's dad met them at the door of his home. It was like he'd been on the lookout for them. He threw the front door open. The motion and noise startled Josh and Todd. They both jumped in place. Mr. Fisher's brow was furrowed. His voice boomed. He said, "You two boys get in here right now."

With the drugs in their systems, Josh and Todd were totally freaked out by Mr. Fisher's manner and words. At first, they couldn't figure out what they might have done wrong. Their walk had gone so well. Then they realized there was a whole host of things they were guilty of. They looked at each other. They each thought about running, but in their states, they couldn't communicate that with their eyes. They bowed their heads, and they followed Mr. Fisher into his home.

Once his door closed, Mr. Fisher said, "I just got off the phone with your mother." He was addressing his words to Josh, but he glared menacingly at Todd as he spoke too. "And she is worried sick about you. She has no idea where you spent last night. She has no idea where you've been this morning. She didn't know if you were alive or dead. And of course my daughter says she hasn't seen or heard from you since last night at the mall, which you and I both know is a lie. Then here you two come laughing and grinning, strolling right up to my front door without a care in the world."

A pit settled into Josh's gut. It opened up a world of anger and fear. He didn't know how he was going to get out of this one. He'd been in so much trouble lately. His mom had been threatening to send him to a psychiatric hospital. She could never discover he was tripping. Josh inhaled deeply. He didn't know why his mom even cared where he was. She was remarried. She had her husband. She didn't need him. Without meaning to, he looked up defiantly at Mr. Fisher who huffed and shook his head.

Mr. Fisher called the boys' parents. Then the three of them—Josh, Todd, and Mr. Fisher—got into the cab of his truck. The two boys didn't even get a chance to see Melody before they left. Mr. Fisher wouldn't allow it. Their friend yelled at her dad about how he couldn't imprison her. She'd get out of there, she shouted from her room at the back of the house. Mr. Fisher shook his head.

The drive was quiet. Mr. Fisher didn't turn on the radio. Josh sat next to him in the middle of the cab's single seat. Todd was on the outside next to the window. He stared at himself in the sideview mirror. His eyes were bugging out of his skull. His trip had taken a turn for the worse. He didn't want to wind up back in that juvenile detention center. He was still on probation.

Josh remained calm. The suburban landscape of houses, strip malls, and trees fluttered away in the windshield. It was consistently being made, unmade, and remade. Josh focused on a sensation in his stomach. It was peace in the midst of insanity. That was a feeling he had to cultivate if he was going to spend eternity in hell. He couldn't be afraid. He needed to remain calm no matter how crazy the world around him became. He would deal with his mom when he finally saw her.

Todd got dropped off at his mom's apartment first. He got out of the truck without saying goodbye to either Mr. Fisher or Josh. He walked up the outside steps to his unit.

Once Todd was inside the door, Mr. Fisher slowly pulled away. He still didn't say anything for the rest of the drive, not until Josh was getting ready to get out of the truck. Then Mr. Fisher turned to his daughter's best friend. Coming off his own recent divorce, he felt it was his responsibility to give the boy some mature advice. He sighed, and he said, "You need to be careful, son. In this world, things can get out of hand real quick."

Josh nodded. He tried being deferential to Mr. Fisher. That seemed like it would be the appropriate response if he were sober, but he couldn't summon the right emotion to his countenance. With a shrug, he got out of the truck. He walked up to his front door without a single glance back at Mr. Fisher who once again was slowly pulling away.

Josh's mom was waiting on a leather chair in the vestibule when Josh came in the front door. "So where were you last night?" she asked him. She looked haggard. She appeared more worn than her 41 years of age should have made her. Josh could tell she'd been smoking cigarettes already that morning. She told people she'd quit smoking four years ago, when Josh was still in fifth grade, before they'd left California. But when things got difficult, she always smelled of tobacco.

It must have had something to do with the drugs coursing through his mind. It might have been an attempt to deflect his mother's anger. It couldn't have had anything to do with how worn down his mom looked, but at that moment, something broke inside of Josh. His mom was sitting in the leather chair that had been her father's, Josh's grandfather's, when he'd been alive. A lump moved into Josh's throat. He swallowed slowly to try and send it back down his esophagus, but that action only brought his emotions deeper into his countenance. His eyes welled up. He sniffled once, and then he burst into tears. They drowned him with heavy waves. Amid the unending surge, Josh said, "I can't live like this anymore."

His mom stood up. She didn't know if she trusted her son. That was a hard feeling to accept. She walked over to him, and she embraced him. Josh cried into his mom's shoulder. She said, "You need to go to that AA meeting again."

Two days later, on a Tuesday night, in the darkness surrounding the church, in the graveyard outside that AA meeting, Josh said to Matt, "Yeah, man, we dropped that acid."

4.

Josh's mother, Annie Gladstone, was in her kitchen that Sunday morning eating a bagel with cream cheese when the phone rang. Bagels weren't a regular culinary item that far south. They didn't even have good bagels available at the grocery stores outside Richmond, but Annie didn't realize that anymore. She was a Jewish girl from Chicago. However, even before Richmond, she'd spent so long in Southern California, she'd forgotten what a good bagel tasted like.

Her husband, Bill, was in the shower. He was getting ready to go to work. He'd mentioned when they were getting in bed the night before that he had some things he wanted to get a jump on before the week started. Annie didn't know what couldn't wait until Monday, but there was no reason not to believe him. He'd started his own company when they'd moved to Louthain three and a half years earlier. In fact, that company was precisely what had brought them all the way across the country. Bill's main investor was located in Potterfield County outside Richmond. That was why they'd moved, and that meant Bill worked more than most. Annie wasn't working herself those days. She'd been a school teacher back in California, but Bill had been supporting them since they'd moved. Annie enjoyed being a stay-at-home wife and mother. Even if she had felt recently like she was going a little stir-crazy. Josh's behavior certainly wasn't helping. She answered the phone, "Hello?"

A woman's voice she didn't recognize said, "Hello? Is this Josh's mother? This is Judy Campbell. I need to speak with Todd if he's awake."

It took a moment for Judy's words to fully register with Annie. Her initial thought when she heard the mother of her son's friend introduce herself was that something had happened to Josh. A wave of fear washed over her. Then as Judy's words became clear, a deeper pit dropped in Annie's stomach. She hadn't expected it but with the way things had been recently, she should have known. She needed to get her facts straight. She wanted to make sure it wasn't a misunderstanding. She said, "I thought the boys were spending the night at your place…"

After she got off the phone with Judy, Annie spent the next two hours frantically calling every number she could find for one of Josh's friends. She wished she'd had Carrie's number, but she didn't. Nobody knew anything. When she heard back from Ronnie Fisher that the two boys had simply wandered up to his house, she finally told Bill to go in to work. He was restless. After Bill left, relieved her son was safe, Annie stepped outside and smoked a cigarette on the back porch. Her husband found tobacco addiction a disgusting habit. He couldn't know she still indulged in it. She put out her cigarette, threw it into the woods, lit another, smoked it, threw that one into the woods, went back inside, washed her hands, and brushed her teeth. Then she sat down in a leather chair by the front door and waited for her son.

After Mr. Fisher had dropped Josh off at home, after his mom told him he needed to go to that AA meeting while staring into the tears streaming down his face, Annie Gladstone was willing to listen to her son's side of the story. He started by telling her how scared he was. He and Todd had only wanted to get away from it all, all the abuse Todd had lived with throughout his life. Josh spent the night in the woods with his friend who wanted to be free. All he wanted was to be free.

"Were you drinking?" Annie asked.

"No," Josh said. He shook his head. By the time he finished his monologue, even he believed his lies.

Annie wanted to believe her son too, but she didn't know if she should. His tears brought a lump into Annie's own throat. She frowned. She wanted to cry as well for everything her son had had to live through over the past few years: her divorce, the death of her father—Josh's grandfather, the dog they'd put to sleep, how poorly Josh got along with Bill. Her new husband was always going on about how Josh needed more discipline. That's what had turned him into the man he'd grown into, Bill said—discipline. "Don't you want Josh to be more like your husband?" Bill asked. Annie wasn't sure.

"But Josh is suffering right now," Annie said, and that day, after Josh got home, she could see it. He was suffering so deeply, and she didn't know what to do to stop it.

She said, "I really think you need to go back to that AA meeting." Annie hoped her son would open up to somebody there in a way he couldn't open up to her or his father or even Dr. Meyer. Her son needed help, and Annie—despite her warnings to Josh—wasn't ready to take Dr. Meyer's advice that the boy might need to be hospitalized.

"I'll go to that meeting," Josh said. "I want to go. It's

a good place." In the moment, Josh really believed what he was saying. LSD was such a strange drug. He smiled at his mom. He loved her.

Even though she didn't want to, his mom smiled back. She needed to maintain a stern exterior, but she was hopeful. She was relieved that her son was safe at home. She'd been afraid something might have happened to him, that she may never see her boy again. But holding him in her arms as he cried that morning, anything seemed possible. She prayed that was the worst it would ever get. It wasn't.

"I need to go upstairs," Josh said, wiping away his tears. "I have homework to do."

Again, Annie was relieved. As far as she could tell, Josh never did his homework. It was as if he were turning over a new leaf. This experience might even start the next chapter in Josh's life, return to her the boy she'd known when they'd lived in California, when Josh's father had still lived with them. Annie loved that little boy she'd known back then. She'd liked that little boy too, and she could still see glimmers of that sweet child in the rageful teenager her son had grown into.

"Okay," Annie said. "We'll talk about this more once you're done."

Josh did have homework to do. That wasn't a lie. Even if he wanted to get away from his mom before she realized he was tripping, he had to write a poem for English class. It was due Monday, the following day. Normally, Josh would scribble something down between classes if he did his homework at all, but under the influence of LSD, there was a certain importance to that moment.

Once he got upstairs into the den, though, Josh realized he didn't know how to write a poem. He set his pen to the paper, but nothing came to mind. He hadn't paid attention to any of the lessons in class. He'd been too busy reading his copy of Anton Szandor LaVey's *Satanic Bible*. He turned on The Doors. They were from the 1960s. That was the heyday of LSD. Teenagers had dropped tab after tab of acid to their music over the years. Maybe Jim Morrison would inspire him. The Doors' singer and lyricist had been a true poet, or so Josh's father had taught him.

Josh didn't put much stock in what most adults had to say. His father, however, was a different story. Even though Josh would never admit that. His father was the keystone missing from Josh's arch. He listened to everything the man said during their weekly phone calls. It was as if his dad's words could teach Josh who he was supposed to be. But he never heard the right things. The answers his father provided were riddles. They never filled the gaping hole Josh felt in his soul. They slipped right out like water through all the cracks in Josh's mind. Instead, Josh looked to the music his father had turned him onto—and the music his father hadn't turned him onto, the music he'd discovered on his own—to teach him what he was supposed to think, how he was supposed to behave.

The singer's lyrics were pulling Josh in. His dad had been right. The dichotomy was stark. Jim Morrison's words meant something. With all their talk about "the other side," they were about exactly where Josh was at, what he was doing, right then. They were about exactly what he'd been doing for the past three and a half years, ever since he'd moved to Virginia and decided he was going to be a metalhead. He didn't want to be the kid he'd been in elementary school any longer, the kid Kevin McComas had always picked on. Just like Jim Morrison sang in the song Josh was listening to right then, he was breaking through to the other side. Was that dangerous?

His mom probably believed it was, but she didn't know anything. Josh wasn't sure. He didn't know what was on the other side. If he was in the light, then it might be the night. If he was in the dark, then it could be the day. It could have been angels. It could have been demons. Josh didn't know which he wanted to meet. In his state, neither seemed safe. It could be God. It could be the devil. It could have been something, or else it was nothing. Josh didn't know.

Instead of writing his poem, Josh lay down on the carpet on his floor. It was the same spot where he'd lost his virginity to Carrie less than four months before. He spread his arms out to either side. He closed his eyes. He was flying. Then a sensation shot through his ankles and his palms. Light lit behind his eyelids…

He was Jesus being nailed to the cross. He'd been caught, beaten, and abused. He could taste the blood on his lips. He could feel the swelling in his eyes. Centurions lifted him up and set him in place. He had a vision from atop the hill of Golgotha. More crosses were set up on either side of him. The sun burned above him. A crowd of mourners gathered below him. Melody, Carrie, and his mother were among them. Melody was the sister of Lazarus. Carrie was Mary Magdalene. His mother was the Divine Virgin. The pain was agonizing. Josh was dying. He would enter the underworld, and he would fight the devil to save his soul. Still lying on the floor of his parents' upstairs den, Josh grimaced. He called on God to save him. He didn't want to be a Satanist anymore. He didn't want to be crucified. He didn't want to die.

5.

The following weekend, Josh was grounded. On Saturday morning, he could talk on the phone, but he still couldn't leave the house. He was used to it. He stayed upstairs in the den, listening to music on his stereo. All the pieces of that stereo had been gifts from his father. Josh was getting really into death metal bands like Deicide and Morbid Angel back then. Earache Records had recently released their UK catalog in the United States. Death metal was quickly overtaking thrash metal as Josh's music of choice. His mother had tried taking his tapes and CDs from him when he'd been grounded before, but that hadn't made a difference. The music wasn't the problem, she'd admitted to herself. Her son was the problem. After depriving the boy of his freedom, there was no need to deprive him of what brought him joy. Bill disagreed, but even if Annie didn't understand what Josh found so uplifting about those dark notes, she knew her son was much more pleasant to be around when he had access to them.

Morbid Angel was worshiping at the *Altars of Madness* when the phone rang. Josh answered before his mother had a chance. Annie figured it was probably for her son anyway. He got more phone calls than she or her husband did. "Hello?" Josh said.

Carrie was crying at the other end of the line. "He's doing it again," she said.

"What?" Josh asked.

"My brother, Isaac, he's starting in with me again," Carrie said.

Like the blind god of chaos—*Azagthoth*—who Morbid Angel worshipped, for a second, Josh lost his sense of sight. Then he gazed clearly out the window at the dead, autumn trees surrounding their home. He said, "I'll be right there."

Josh hung up the phone. He called Ben, a friend of theirs who had a car. He'd dated Melody in the past, but they'd broken up after a single kiss. Ben still held a resentment toward Josh's best friend for that short romance. Josh usually shrugged when Ben brought up Melody under his breath and cursed her through the songs he dedicated to her as he drove Josh around Potterfield County while Josh drank beer after beer and shot after shot of Everclear. Ben didn't drink. Josh never knew why.

"I need you to pick me up, man," Josh said. Right then he didn't care that he was grounded. Carrie needed help. She needed somebody to save her. She needed Josh.

Josh sat by the window in his family's upstairs den until Ben's Pontiac Phoenix pulled up in front of his house. The last time Josh had ridden with Ben had been on a Friday night on their way back from the mall and Dave's, the pool hall across the street. That night, as usual, Josh had been drunk. He'd thrown up out Ben's window. He'd splattered the exterior of the Phoenix with chunks of vomit. When he reminded Josh of that at the mall the following week, Ben laughed about cleaning it all off the side of his usually pristine car, but Josh could tell his friend wasn't thrilled with the mess he'd made.

Through the den's glass window, the autumn sun lit the side of Josh's face with a warmth that didn't exist outside. The trees cast black shadows that cut across the gray road. Josh kept one eye on those shadows. He didn't want to miss Ben pulling up. He didn't want his mom to know he was planning on leaving that afternoon. She would try to stop him. There would be an argument. She might even call Bill who—at 6'6"—was big enough to make sure Josh couldn't go anywhere, and Josh needed to get out of the house that day. His mom could never understand. She was too implanted in her own world. He needed to help Carrie.

As soon as Josh saw Ben's car coming up the road, he grabbed his leather jacket out of his bedroom. Ben's car passed in and out of the trees' shadowed leaves dancing in the fall breeze. Running downstairs and out the door, Josh slipped into his jacket. He met Ben as he pulled up in front of his home. He didn't wait for him to say anything. He hopped in the passenger seat, and he said, "We need to get Todd. We're going to Carrie's."

Annie was reading a book in the living room when her son came bounding down the steps. Hoping he was coming to speak with her, that he had something he wanted to share with her, she set her book aside. The front door opened and closed. Josh didn't even try to be discreet. "Josh?" she asked. He didn't answer. Annie stood up. Out the front window, Ben's car pulled away with Josh in the passenger seat. A confused expression passed across Annie's face. A pit sank into her gut.

Todd already knew Josh was on his way. Josh had called him too. Unlike Josh, however, Todd wasn't grounded. He could still do anything he wanted. He could still go anywhere he could get. It wasn't that Todd's mom didn't want to discipline her son. For her to try simply seemed pointless. She would never be able to enforce any semblance of authority she attempted to implement. She was always at work.

Neither Todd nor Ben, though, knew the real reason why they were going to Carrie's. Josh had promised his girlfriend he would never reveal to anyone else the full extent of her private suffering. All the other boys knew was that her 17-year-old brother, Isaac, had hit her, which in reality was only a fraction of what was happening. But even with the small amount of information available to him, Todd was ready to fight the older brother at Josh's side.

Ben intended to drop the two of them off and leave. He wasn't about to get into a fight that day. He was small and thin. He walked a little hunched over. Besides, he'd seen Isaac before. Along with Carrie's oldest brother, Marcus, Isaac lifted weights every day to rap artists like Big Daddy Kane, Slick Rick, and Eric B. & Rakim. With no other man in the house, Marcus—at 19 years old—was the *de facto* father of the family. He worked construction. He and Isaac were both massive, and they didn't like metalheads. Mainly because the metalheads at their schools had never liked them. The metalheads had always called the two white brothers variations on racial epithets—words the two brothers found offensive in their own rights, but when directed at them, always led to a fight.

Josh said they'd give Ben a call when they were ready to head home. There was a payphone at the top of Carrie's neighborhood. Josh couldn't go to any of his friends' places to make the call. His mom might have already been in touch with any number of their parents looking for him.

Ben said that was fine. He even gave Josh a quarter. He'd just bought *Horrorscope,* the new Overkill album, which he played for Josh and Todd during the drive over to Carrie's. He hadn't had a chance to listen to the whole thing yet. He wanted to spend the rest of the afternoon in his bedroom really digging into those songs.

As they approached Carrie's house from around the corner where Ben had dropped them off, Josh had no idea what he and Todd were planning to do. It was like he was back in his parents' living room in California watching some movie about greasers in the 1950s. Only he was living the main character's life. They were acting on instinct, instincts learned from those same movies Josh had watched back in California. Josh hadn't even had anything to drink yet that day. He was trembling from a mixture of adrenaline and fear.

Todd was telling Josh what their plan was. They would head around back, sneak in through the back door, find Isaac watching TV on the couch, and jump him right there in the middle of his own home. He wouldn't even know what was happening. Todd had never met either of Carrie's brothers. He wasn't afraid. He said he'd done this kind of thing before. He had "experience" with this kind of situation.

The two metalheads walked down the road, hunched over like coyotes on the prowl. Josh kept glancing every which way as if he expected somebody to be on them at any moment. Like the coyote he appeared to be, it was as if he believed he was the hunted rather than the hunter. As much as he needed to defend Carrie, he'd never been in a fight like the one they were approaching before, one where an adult might not break it up before it got out of hand, but he'd forgotten that. Like Todd, he was trying to act as if he engaged in this kind of behavior all the time, but somewhere deeper in his soul, he knew the truth. His body language couldn't lie. As much as he wanted to believe he was, he wasn't living in a movie.

The two boys were approaching Carrie's chain link fence when Marcus spotted them out the back window. Things were a madhouse inside his mother's home. He'd gone out that morning to run some errands. His mom was at work, and when he got home, his baby sister was in the bathroom with a knife, threatening to slice her own face. "I don't want to be pretty anymore," she'd screamed.

Isaac was nowhere to be found. Marcus had no idea what was happening, but he figured it had something to do with that white trash boy the little girl was dating.

Marcus held Carrie as she cried on his shoulder, but she wouldn't tell him what had happened. He convinced her to get into bed and go to sleep, but he had no idea what was going on between her and their other brother underneath his mother's roof. When he saw Josh and his friend creeping up to their back fence, he stormed out into the yard. He shouted, "What are you two doing here?"

The two metalheads stopped dead in their tracks on the other side of the fence. "Is that him?" Todd asked.

Josh shook his head, *No.*

Enraged, Marcus charged the fence like a bull in his paddock. He said, "I don't know what you did to my little sister, but I found her in the bathroom threatening to cut up her own face. If you set one foot on my property, I'll break your neck."

Josh believed Marcus, and he had no quarrel with the oldest brother. Besides, if Marcus was home, Carrie would be safe from Isaac. Josh didn't need to do anything. If Marcus would let them leave, there didn't have to be a fight. Josh didn't want to admit it, but he was relieved about that. Throughout their drive, he'd reflected on the rashness of his decision and his unpreparedness for the result. He put his hands up in a gesture of peace. In as conciliatory a manner as possible, he said, "I'm just trying to help Carrie, man. That's all."

Marcus didn't understand what the boy was talking about. As far as he could tell, everything was that hillbilly's fault. As quickly as a copperhead, he stepped toward the fence again. Even Todd jumped back as if he were afraid he was about to get bitten. Marcus pointed one finger at the two metalheads. He said, "You're not helping anything, man, and if I ever catch you near my little sister again, I'll kill you."

Josh bowed his head. Marcus was serious. As he heaved with breath, it was apparent the man hated his baby sister's boyfriend. Josh swallowed slowly. Keeping his hands in the air, he stepped away from the fence. As if sudden movements might rekindle the situation, he wanted to appear as unthreatening as possible. He wondered—if Marcus really had turned against him— whether he would ever see Carrie again. He wanted to cry.

As the two boys walked back up the same road they'd come down, Todd asked, "So what do you want to do now?"

Josh shrugged. "Well, I can't go home," he said. "Let's call Ben and head up to the mall."

6.

Josh was drunk in the backseat of Ben's Phoenix. Moonlight streamed over his shoulders. It lit his hair hanging down over the back of his neck. Todd was sitting on his left. Somebody else was on his right. He was trapped in the middle. The person to his right was holding his head in his hands. He looked like he might puke any moment now. Josh felt claustrophobic. He wanted to scream. He needed to scream. He screamed—

Ben had picked Josh and Todd up from a corner store across the street from Carrie's neighborhood. It was right next to the church where Josh had gone to that AA meeting the previous Tuesday night. Then the three of them drove to the mall. Ben kept trying to turn Josh onto that new Overkill album. The two of them had always bonded over music before, and this was right up the younger headbanger's alley. But Josh wasn't in the mood for music right then.

Nothing was really happening at the mall though. So after Ben bought Josh and Todd something to eat—unlike the two younger teenagers, Ben had a job—the three metalheads headed across the street to Dave's. Even though it was only about 5:00 in the evening, Dave's had a lot more going on. Todd got some quarters from Ben and put them on one of the pool tables for a game. Josh took a seat in the back corner. Unlike his friends, he didn't know how to shoot pool. Even though he believed he should. It fit his image.

Josh slouched down in his chair. He couldn't go home. He didn't know where he would spend the night. The weekend before, he and Todd had proven it was too cold to sleep outside, and he couldn't set foot back on Carrie's property. Marcus had made sure of that. Josh kicked the table in front of him. It bucked in place. Some metalhead he didn't know shot him a nasty glance. Josh stared back at the older kid until the older kid muttered something underneath his breath, shook his head, and looked away. Josh kept staring in that kid's direction. He cursed himself for not protecting Carrie, and he wished he had something to drink. He rubbed his forehead. He wanted to take his insecurities and frustrations out on everyone in that place.

It didn't take long before a friend of Carrie's, a girl named Amber, invited Josh and Todd out to the parking lot with her and her boyfriend, Chris, to share a bottle of grape MD 20/20, Mad Dog wine, and a case of beer. Chris had a car. Josh didn't know the make or model. The four of them piled into it. Amber and Chris were up front. Josh and Todd were in the back.

"So where's Carrie tonight?" Amber asked. Chris unscrewed the cap on their bottle of wine.

"She stayed in," Josh said. His manner was curt. He didn't smile. If Carrie had been in a similar situation to Josh right then, Josh would have been so jealous that a fight between the two teenagers would have been unavoidable.

"Well, tell her I said, 'Hey,' next time you see her," Amber said. Then she asked, "You guys want to smoke? We scored some pot earlier." Chris looked over at his girlfriend. It was obvious she'd overstepped her bounds.

But before Chris could say, *I don't think that's a good idea,* Josh and Todd both said, "Sure."

The four headbangers drank and smoked and talked in the parking lot while they listened to Skid Row's most recent album, *Slave to the Grind.* Josh didn't care much for Skid Row anymore. He remembered a trip to a beach in North Carolina with his mom and stepdad a few years before. Bill's business partner owned the place. He'd rented it to them for the weekend as a welcome to the east coast present. Coming from California, though, that North Carolina beach was pretty depressing. All Josh had done was sit in their hotel room listening to Skid Row's first self-titled album. He'd never even heard the most recent one. He asked, "Can we listen to something else?"

"Sure," Chris said. He slipped the cassette out of the tape deck and put a different one in. The music's bass and drums quickly gave way to a lead guitar that turned into Axl Rose's high-pitched wail. Guns N Roses was the first band that had opened Josh's mind to heavy metal back in fifth grade, but things were different then.

Josh shook his head, "Christ, man? Don't you have any metal?"

Chris bristled at Josh's words. "This is metal," he said above the hard rock blaring out of his speakers.

"No," Josh said, "I mean real metal like Megadeth or Slayer—"

"I don't listen to any of that stuff."

Josh shook his head. "How can you not listen to Slayer?" he asked.

"I don't like all their Satanic stuff," Chris said. "I'm a

Christian."

Josh laughed. "And I'm a Satanist."

"That's not funny," Chris said.

He turned around in the front seat. He glared at Josh.

"I'm serious," Josh said. "I'm a Satanist."

There was a pause. Chris's gaze went blank. Then something lit behind his eyes. He exploded. "Get out of my car."

Josh didn't move. Chris lunged at him from the front seat. He swung and popped Josh across the cheek. Josh's head spun. He whipped his neck back and glared at the older kid still staring him down.

"Please get out of the car, Josh," Amber said. She was pleading and sincere.

Still staring at Chris huffing in the driver's seat, Josh opened the door and got out. As Josh stepped onto the pavement, Chris yelled once more without getting out of the car, "And get to a church, boy. You're going to burn in hell."

Stoned and buzzed, standing on the curb as Todd stumbled toward him from the car's other side, Josh shook his head. He rubbed his jaw. It didn't hurt like he'd thought it would. In fact, between the evening's alcohol and marijuana, it didn't feel like anything—

"Jesus Christ, will you be quiet," Ben said from the front seat of his Phoenix. To Josh's left, Todd laughed. Josh realized he was screaming in the backseat of Ben's car as the moonlight shone over his shoulders. He'd shared a bottle of Everclear with somebody, but he couldn't remember who it was.

"What's wrong with you?" the guy on his right mumbled.

"I'm a Satanist," Josh said. "I need to be saved."

The guy to his right shook his head.

"I can feel the flames," Josh continued. "They're burning me from the inside. Oh, God—" He screamed again.

"Will you please shut up?" Ben said once more. The girl in the passenger seat turned and looked Josh square in the eye. She didn't look anything like Melody or that girl from the meeting. She had dark, almost black hair with bags under her eyes and rouge all over her cheeks.

Josh didn't recognize her. He really could feel the flames of hell. They were hot and cold at the same time. They scorched his insides like an unending shot of whisky. They froze his soul as if his skin had sloughed away and exposed his nerves to the night air from the weekend before. He was the grass on a lawn simultaneously brittle from a morning frost and scorched from the noonday sun. "Help me," Josh said.

Ben shook his head. The girl in the passenger seat turned back to face the front…

Josh was sitting in the backseat of a parked car. Nobody was on either side of him.

He remembered asking to be taken to a church where he could talk to a priest. That must have been where he was now in the dark at 10:30 pm on a Saturday night. Everybody else was inside. They were in the confessional being forgiven.

Josh jumped out of the car. He couldn't miss the opportunity. He didn't recognize Todd's apartment complex before him. He didn't notice the guy who had been sitting to his right—the guy he didn't remember sharing that bottle of Everclear with—puking in the gutter next to the car. He definitely didn't recognize the girl from the front seat, and he didn't hear Ben shout, "Josh!" as he took off for the nearest streetlight leading him to what he believed was the priest's door.

The lights led him on. He stumbled and weaved up the sidewalk. He banged on the priest's door with enough force to wake the dead. "Help me!" he shouted. "I need to be saved," he said over and over again. All the while he banged on the door, lights clicked on from all the porches surrounding him. A woman's face peered out the window beside him. Josh wasn't aware of any of it. The door flew open.

A man appeared in his bathrobe. He was holding something long and dark in his right hand, but Josh didn't know what it was. That man had to be the priest. He couldn't be anybody else. Josh tried to rush past him to the altar in the church. There, the priest could bless him with holy water. He could save his soul from the flames of hell. Josh had already sold his soul to the devil.

He'd written a letter backward in English. He'd pledged his earthly being and afterlife to the forces of evil because he hated "the good." He'd burn in hell before he'd join humanity in heaven. He would defeat the Lord. He would destroy the world. He would annihilate the spirit. He burned that letter upon an altar and scattered its ashes to the four winds.

"I need you to save me," Josh said to the priest.

"What are you talking about?" the priest asked. He shoved Josh back out his door. He was looking around, stepping in place, closing his bathrobe with his left hand, and holding that long, dark thing—whatever it was—in his right hand.

"I need your help," Josh said. "I'm a Satanist. You need to save me. It's your job." Josh moved to get past the priest again, but the priest blocked his door one more time.

"The hell it is," the priest said. He shoved Josh back along the path. Josh stumbled. He fell. When he stood back up, weaving in place, Josh was looking down the dark barrel of a shotgun. The priest's eyes were open behind the sight.

Josh didn't understand why the priest was pointing a gun at him. He pushed the barrel out of his face. A surprised look appeared on the priest's face as the man stared at his weapon pointing toward the ground. "But you have to help me," Josh said. "You're a priest."

"No, I'm not," the priest said. But Josh didn't hear him. The man raised the shotgun once more to Josh's face. He pumped it once. A bullet chambered. A woman came running out the door. She screamed and grabbed the man's arm. Josh tried getting around the priest again. If he could make it to the altar himself, he could beg the Lord for forgiveness.

But the priest swung his right arm and caught Josh with his fist on the cheek below the eye. Josh fell down to the ground again. The woman was crawling up the priest's back now. He was shouting at her and shoving her off. Josh rubbed the bruise swelling around his eye. He never expected to get hit in the face by a priest.

7.

The world was fluid. It rolled in and out like the waves that had knocked Josh down as a toddler running along a California beach. His father picked him up, set him on his shoulders, and let him scan the distant horizon. The sky melted into the ocean. Sometimes, nothing was there. Then another wave came, and it was all miraculous again. Josh's eyes grew wide. In those moments, he could only see a few inches in front of his face. The rest of the world didn't exist.

He sat slouched over a table. His left eye was swollen, but he couldn't feel it. His lips were puffed up from when he'd jumped back up and tried getting past the priest one more time. But he couldn't feel that either. The man had grabbed Josh by his black tee shirt. He'd ripped the neck down the front and hit Josh in the face two more times. Then Ben came and put his arm over Josh's shoulder. He walked the younger kid away from the man in the bathrobe holding a shotgun and shouting at Josh to, "Get away from my home!" Ben put Josh in the backseat of his car, and he drove him away from Todd's apartment complex and back to Dave's Pool Hall.

But Josh didn't remember any of that. He didn't know how he'd wound up sitting there once again at that table where he'd already been sitting with a worthless game of pool he could barely see going on in front of him.

Then he noticed the stride of a familiar gait gliding through the pool hall. It was Bill Gladstone, Josh's stepdad, making his way through the smoky throng. Still sporting a mustache from his disco days in the late seventies, Bill towered above the teenage and twenty-something metalheads and rednecks bent over the pool tables. He looked every which way. His eyes lit on Josh sitting still at that table he'd been packing another cigarette at for God knows how long.

Bill's eyes widened then narrowed as he strode toward Josh, but Josh didn't wait. He stood up. He nodded at the other two drunks who he didn't know sitting at the table with him.

"Well, I've got to go now," he said. He waved goodbye to the twenty-something billiards players who didn't know him either, and he stumbled over to meet up with Bill as if the man were picking him up from a movie he'd bought his stepson a ticket to earlier.

Bill Gladstone already wasn't in the best mood. He'd been called away from his personal business earlier that day by his wife. Josh had stormed out of the house that afternoon. The boy had already been grounded once again for a week, and he had another week to go. Annie didn't know what to do. She wanted to stay at home in case her son came back, and she wanted Bill to scour the area to try and find him.

Bill had been doing that all day. He'd driven from the mall to Josh's girlfriend's neighborhood and back to the mall. He'd ducked into Dave's, Louthain's one pool hall, every couple of hours. He'd headed back home only to find out Annie knew nothing either. Bill was at his wits' end. He was scared for Josh and angry with him at the same time. If he found the boy, he had no idea what he was going to do.

Bill was from the mountains of upstate New York. He'd wanted to be a minister as a child. He'd preached sermons to the winds blowing off the craggy cliffs, but the ways of the world had diverted him from that calling. He tried raising Josh with the same discipline his father had raised him with, but he also wanted to be more approachable than his own father—a Korean War veteran—had ever been.

Bill pointed out attractive women to the boy as they drove around town. When he'd been a teenager, Bill thought he might have wanted an elder to relate to him in the same way. But he also wanted the boy to work hard and be respectful. However, when he'd asked Josh to rake the lawn the year before, the teenager had broken the families' two rakes against a tree and then said he wouldn't be able to complete the task.

When Bill finally saw Josh sitting at a table in the back of that smoky pool hall, it was past 11:30 at night. He'd been looking for his stepson for nearly seven hours by then. He was immediately struck by how Josh's tee shirt was ripped down the front. Bruises covered the boy's face. Josh's left eye was nearly swollen shut. His lips were puffed out. He'd been hit repeatedly. Bill's eyes grew wide. He'd never been in a fight himself. There'd been shoving matches in locker rooms and on basketball courts, but he'd never been beaten up. He was quite a bit taller than most men, and that made him intimidating. He'd never assaulted another as it now appeared Josh had been either. As he realized the boy was probably drunk leaning back in his chair, rage curdled in Bill's gut. He narrowed his eyes.

He needed to appear stern when Josh noticed him.

"Hey, Bill," Josh said. He waved as he approached his stepdad.

"Don't 'Hey, Bill,' me," Bill said. The boy wasn't walking straight. He was slurring his words. He was far too nonchalant for the situation. "We're getting out of here right now."

"I know," Josh said. "I already said goodbye."

In Bill's luxury sedan, they drove in silence. There wasn't any music on. Josh looked out the window. Everything went by so fast. In the darkness, the suburban landscape merged into an unending blur reminding Josh of how the world was when he stood still in his current state. Josh laughed. He didn't know if he was moving. He bobbed to the bumps in the road. His head lolled on his neck. He appeared like he might pass out, but he stayed straight in his seat. Glancing to his right, Bill gripped the wheel tighter. He shook his head. As they pulled into their own neighborhood, Bill finally said, "Your mother and I were worried sick about you."

"Why?" Josh asked. He was still looking out the window.

It took Bill a second to make out the word Josh had slurred. When he did, he took a deep breath. He repositioned his hands on the steering wheel, and he said, "I don't know why you wouldn't think we'd be worried about you. You've been missing all day."

"It's not like you care," Josh said.

"I care. Your mom cares," Bill said. "You're our responsibility."

"Why don't you act like it sometime," Josh said.

Rage boiled over in Bill's gut. He slammed on the brakes in the middle of the street. Nobody was behind them, but if there'd been somebody there, he would have slammed straight into the back of Bill's car. Somebody would have gotten hurt. At that time of night, though, in that neighborhood, it was a safe bet nobody was out. "Take a look at yourself, Josh," Bill said. "If you cared about your mom, you wouldn't be acting like this. You'd show me the respect I deserve, and you wouldn't leave your mom crying on the couch all day. You'd—"

Josh spun around in his seat. His eyes burned. Smoke fumed from his nose. Fire shot out of his mouth. He said, "Don't tell me how I need to act. You don't care about me, and you don't care about my family. You're just in this for my mom—"

Bill's hands shot off the steering wheel. He grabbed Josh by the front of his torn tee shirt. He pulled Josh close to his face, "You listen to me, now—"

"Let go," Josh screamed. He pulled away from Bill's grasp. His already ripped tee shirt almost tore into two pieces down the front of his chest. Josh threw open the passenger side door. He leaped out of the parked car. "I'll walk," he said, and he slammed the passenger door closed again.

Bill sat still for a moment staring into the darkness. He didn't know how everything had devolved so quickly. Even though he hadn't struck the boy as his father might have done to him, Bill was embarrassed he'd laid a hand on his wife's son. Even if it had been only to grab the boy's tee shirt. He stared at Josh standing alone outside the car and weaving in place. The boy was in bad shape. Bill shook his head. He rolled down the passenger side window. "Get back in the car," he said.

"Go to hell."

Bill didn't try convincing his stepson to get back in the car again. He shifted his car into gear, and he drove off alone. He didn't know what he would tell his wife once he got home.

8.

When Josh and his mom had still lived in Southern California, when both their last names had still been Marshall, Josh loved his mom's new boyfriend, Bill Gladstone. Before dating his mom, Bill had been Josh's basketball coach. It gave Josh a certain cache with his teammates to be almost related to their coach. He'd never been very popular throughout elementary school, and he'd never been very good at sports either. But for some reason, Josh believed he might finally become a basketball star. As if Bill's talents could be translated to him through his own proximity to the man.

Josh and Bill had run a father/son relay race together. They hadn't won, but they had a photo of themselves together with their entry numbers around their necks. Bill bent down. He was almost on the same level as Josh. As if his parents' split had never occurred, Josh appeared rejuvenated. He and Bill were both smiling. Josh even remembered a trip he was going to take to Chicago to visit his grandparents in fifth grade. Before leaving for the airport, Bill had called the airline to make sure his "son's" flight was on time. Josh had swelled with pride at how his mom's fiancé had referred to him.

But that trip was the last time Josh ever saw his mother's father. Josh's grandfather died of a sudden heart attack a few months later. And when Bill moved Josh and his mom all the way across the country to open his new business in Potterfield County outside Richmond, VA, he stopped coaching Josh's basketball team. His new venture took up too much of his time. Josh was left to fend for himself. On some level, he never forgave his new stepdad for that. He quit playing basketball the following year.

Josh weaved up the road. The moonlight lit his way, but he didn't know that. He could almost see where he was going, but no memory was being imprinted on his mind. He'd blacked out. The liquor had made him blind. He was feeling his way instinctually. He stumbled, but he caught himself before tumbling into the ditch beside the road. Nothing more than the walking dead, he might as well have been a zombie.

Josh was cursing and mumbling to himself as he walked. He was fighting with nobody. As if the light itself were his enemy, he was punching the moonlight through the empty air. With nothing mirroring his violence, Josh felt an invisible God laughing at him. By the time he made it home, his spirit was on fire, lit by the burning flames of the 190-proof liquor he'd consumed. Josh was in hell. He was enraged at everyone and everything. He threw open the front door, and he shouted, "Bill Gladstone, I'm going to kill you."

In the kitchen, when the front door flew open and Josh shouted his threat, Annie said to Bill, "Get into the bedroom right now."

Her husband obeyed. He ran down the hall to the master bedroom, and he closed and locked the door. Neither of the adults wanted the teenager to attack the man, and neither of them wanted the man to have to defend himself against the teenager.

Annie immediately picked up the phone and dialed 9-1-1. Tears were in the back of her throat. She'd never had to call the police on her son before. She'd never had to call the police on anyone before. She didn't know what would happen, but she didn't know what else to do.

When the dispatcher picked up, Annie said into the phone, "My son is threatening my husband."

"How old is your son, ma'am?" the dispatcher asked.

"He's 14," Annie said. "He'll be 15 in a week and a half."

At the mention of Josh's birthday, Annie stiffened her face to hold back the tears moving into her eyes. It was no time to cry. But Annie hadn't bought a present for her son yet. Josh had never told her what he wanted. She'd planned on asking him again that weekend, but he'd disappeared before she got the chance.

"We'll send somebody right over," the dispatcher said.

"Thank you," Annie said. She hung up the phone.

"Where is he, Mom?" Josh slurred as he stumbled into the kitchen. He fell against the island in the center, but he caught himself before tumbling to the ground. As he stood back up, Annie noticed Josh's shirt was ripped almost in half. He didn't have his leather jacket with him. His left eye was nearly swollen shut, and his lip was a bloody protrusion. Bill hadn't been exaggerating. Her little boy had gotten beaten up.

Annie steeled herself against her tears. "He's not here, right now," she said as calmly as she could manage. She moved around the kitchen island to get closer to her son.

"That's not true," Josh said. He flung his arms out to keep his mom away from him. He almost fell again. Annie stepped back into safety on the other side of the island.

"I know he's here. Bill!" Josh shouted. He grabbed a

knife out of the block on the counter, and he took off down the hall. Annie screamed.

By the time the two police cars arrived, Josh was sitting out on the front porch crying. The knife was at his feet. It had never been used. With the knife in one hand, Josh had pounded on his parents' bedroom door. "Bill!" he'd shouted over and over again. He'd collapsed in a mess of tears. His mother had grabbed him by the shoulders, and she'd weaved him back out to the front porch.

Wondering what might be going on outside, Bill was hiding alone in the master bedroom. Gravel crunched in the driveway as the police cruisers pulled up. Their headlights shone through the bedroom window.

Josh's mother was beside her son on the steps. "He doesn't love us like dad did, Mom," Josh said.

He still slurred his words. Annie put her arm around her son. He heaved a sob.

With their spotlights shining on the front of the house, the police cars parked in the driveway. Two officers stepped out. With his right hand on the butt of his pistol, one officer cautiously approached the woman and her son. He shone his flashlight into their faces. "Are you okay, ma'am?" he asked.

Annie shielded her eyes. She nodded at the redheaded officer. Josh hung his head. He was still blubbering.

"This is your son?"

Annie nodded again.

"And where is your husband, ma'am?"

"He's inside," Annie said. Josh continued crying. At his mother's words, he dropped his fist against the step he was sitting on. Annie pulled him closer.

"Your husband is all right, then, ma'am?" the officer asked.

Annie nodded, *Yes*.

As Josh cried on the steps beside his mother, the second officer went inside to check on the state of Annie's home. Annie discussed her son's fate with the officer still standing at the base of the steps leading up to her front door. The officer looked at Josh with compassion. With his mother's approval, the officer decided he would take the boy to Safe Haven, a psychiatric hospital north of the city of Richmond. They had an adolescent ward there, and it wasn't as dangerous as a state hospital. The family's insurance would probably cover it. Without much cajoling, Josh agreed to go.

Josh said goodbye to his mom. He hugged her, and he stumbled off to get into the backseat of the police cruiser. It wasn't until after the car pulled away with her son in it that Annie started crying. Like a criminal, Josh's silhouette was reflected in the rear window. Annie stood on the front porch. She cupped her hands around her face. She started sobbing. She didn't get Bill right away, and she didn't know why. She should have wanted her husband with her. Soon, she would go down to the police precinct. As the police officer had directed, she was going to take out what was referred to as a "green warrant" on her son. It would state that Josh was "a danger to himself and others." It would have him committed.

II.

9.

At breakfast the next morning, the other boys in Safe Haven held muted conversations with one another. There'd been mumbles and nods, but nobody had said anything to Josh. They'd glanced at him out of the corners of their eyes. It was as if there was some great secret that they all had knowledge of but that they could never let Josh know. In truth, they were sizing him up, trying to figure out what had happened to him the night before.

After breakfast, Josh sat down in a cushioned chair in the middle of the boys' side of Safe Haven's adolescent unit. He blew his hair out of his throbbing eye, and he stared up at the institution's suspended ceiling. Visions of movies where a teenager like him might make a break for it through a ceiling like that popped into Josh's mind. He pictured himself crawling through air conditioning ducts to safety. He ran through the woods to find Todd, Carrie, and Melody back in their own neighborhoods. Then they all ran away to Los Angeles together. Todd and Josh started a band. They became famous. But Hollywood was only a fantasy. Safe Haven was reality.

Another long haired kid who'd been with them at breakfast sat down on the couch next to Josh's chair. His hair was longer and stringier than Josh's, and it was flaming red. His face and arms were freckled. He was rail thin with black jeans and a white tee shirt. Like all the other boys, he wasn't wearing any shoes, only white socks. There was a hole through his left ear where an earring must have dangled when he was on the outside. "You play chess?" he asked.

Josh nodded. He'd learned chess as a kid from his grandfather.

"Cool. Let's play a game," the redheaded guy said. He smiled. "I'm David."

"Josh," Josh said, and the two of them walked over to a circular table in the corner of the room where a cheap, plastic chess set lay strewn about.

"I'll be white," David said as they sat down.

"That means you go first," Josh said. He didn't mind. He preferred black. It was his favorite color.

"That's fine," David said. He pushed his hair out of his face, and he started setting up the pieces on his side of the board. Across from him, Josh did the same with the black pieces.

The chess pieces were piled haphazardly beside the board. The last players had paid no regard to rank or color. Josh and David started picking through them and setting one army against the other on opposite sides of the board.

"You ready?" David asked. Josh nodded. David made his first move. His king's pawn hopped forward two spaces. Josh countered by moving his kingside knight's pawn forward a single space.

"Where are you from?" David asked.

"Potterfield," Josh said. "You?"

"Althea."

Josh had heard his parents mention the county, but he didn't know exactly where it was. He thought it might be even farther out of the city than where he was in

Potterfield. He nodded, though, like he knew the area better than he did. But his family wasn't from there. He hadn't grown up there. His home was in Southern California. His roots there went back three generations. To Josh, that seemed like a long time.

"You like metal?" David asked in between their next moves.

Josh nodded. "Yeah," he said. He didn't take his eyes off the board.

"Who's your favorite band?" David asked.

"I don't know," Josh said. "These days, probably Deicide or Morbid Angel. I'm a Satanist."

David nodded. "I'm a Nazi," he said.

Josh looked up. Even though his mother's family in Chicago was Jewish, he took the comment in stride. He tilted his head to the side. David was smiling. There was a connection between Nazism and the occult. Josh knew that. The Nazi party had conducted all sorts of magical rituals. Josh knew that. Even the founder of Josh's favorite Satanic sect had admitted a fascination with Nazism. Josh knew that as well. As angry as he was right then about everything, Josh shrugged. He moved his knight up two spaces and over one.

David smiled and made his next move as well. "So what happened to your face?" he asked.

"My stepdad beat me up," Josh said. The night before was a mass of confusing images. Josh couldn't keep his stepdad and the preacher straight. Whatever each had done to him, he didn't know. But he blamed Bill for all of it. He angled his anger toward that one man. It never occurred to him that—like during the Salem Witch Trials—if he kept telling his story the way he was, his stepdad might wind up in prison.

"Damn, man, he really did a number on you," David

said. He moved his bishop out from behind a wall of pawns and placed it in the middle of the board to assert control.

Josh paused to study the game's progress. He castled with his rook and king. It was a defensive move. "I hardly remember it," he said.

As if he didn't know either what to say or how to say it, David's jaw dropped open. A nonplussed expression creased his features. But he had to keep his cool. He made his next move. "You must have been pretty wasted," he said.

Josh shrugged. "Pretty much."

"What were you on?"

"Weed and alcohol."

"Must have been a lot."

"It was Everclear."

David nodded as if he knew what that was, but he didn't. He'd never heard stories about what the grain alcohol could do to somebody—damage their brains, make them go blind. Josh wasn't paying attention though. He was contemplating his next move in their chess match. He didn't understand the game well enough yet to know that without even realizing it, he'd already won.

As he studied the board, an outside voice broke into Josh's thoughts. "You guys mind if I get winner?" Josh looked across the table at David to get his new friend's opinion, but David was glaring at the person standing over Josh's shoulder. Josh followed David's stare. He glanced up and to his right. A black kid was standing there looking down at the two metalheads' game.

"We don't play games with your kind," David said.

A quizzical expression creased the black kid's features. He said, "What's that supposed to mean?"

"You know what it means," David said. He narrowed

his eyes.

Josh could almost hear the racial slur that David intended to follow his sentence. Josh's heart started racing. He looked down at the game they were playing together. He brought his shoulders up. His palms sweat. His cheeks burned.

The black kid slammed his fist down on the table. With a crash of black and white pieces, David and Josh's game was upended. It scattered across the table and onto the floor. "Don't talk to me like that," the kid said.

"I'll talk to you however I please," David said, flicking his hair out of his eyes. He didn't stand up, but his neck twisted like a slithering snake.

"Is there a problem over there?" somebody shouted from the other side of the room. Josh looked back over his shoulder. A staff member was approaching them.

"No problem here," the black kid said. "We were just talking about who was playing the next game."

The black kid backed away from Josh and David, but he kept his stare glued to David. David picked a stray strand of hair from in front of his eye. He looked back down at the board. The headbangers' game was ruined. Pieces lay scattered every which way. As they moved to pick them up, Josh noticed David's hands were trembling.

10.

Days were pretty much all the same at Safe Haven. Every morning, a staff member woke Josh up at 7:00 am. He got dressed and got in line to walk down the hall to breakfast where there was a boy's table and a girl's table. Patients could talk at breakfast, but they didn't say much. There wasn't much to talk about. Besides, it was early. The easiest way to start an argument was to try beginning a conversation with somebody who wasn't fully awake yet. And even with the staff members surrounding them, arguments could escalate pretty quickly.

After breakfast, all the kids went to their morning groups. There, they were divided into whether they abused substances or not. The kids who abused substances were called the CD—chemically dependent—group. The kids who didn't abuse substances were called the non-CD—non-chemically dependent—group. Josh was placed in the CD group. In group, they were supposed to get in touch with how they felt about being in Safe Haven, what had brought them there, and why they'd started abusing substances in the first place.

Josh didn't say anything. He listened. He knew that wouldn't get him out of there any faster, but he didn't care. It didn't matter what they'd used or how much they'd used. If they were using substances as teenagers, the doctors placed them in the CD group. The goal was to get the kids to admit they were either alcoholics or drug addicts. Josh had no problem admitting that. He knew it, but he didn't want to change. After everything he'd been through, his plan for after he got out of that place was to drink himself to death.

Then there was school. The kids had to go to school there too. Josh's teachers from Louthain High School sent him assignments every Monday. His teacher at Safe Haven sent them back out to be graded every Friday. Josh never found out how he was performing. He simply sat quietly in class every day and did his work.

After school, there was lunch, afternoon group, some free time in the gym—when Josh sat on a weight bench talking with David. They didn't lift weights. They only talked about heavy metal. Then there was more school, dinner—which was more talkative than breakfast or lunch, and some quiet time around the unit when Josh would play chess. He was the best player there. Before long, the only patient who would play him was David, and that was more for conversation than anything else. Josh had no idea how that had happened. He'd never been very good at chess when he'd been a kid. But he was the Grandmaster of Safe Haven. The few lessons he'd had from his grandfather had certainly paid off. Finally, the kids had an evening small group right before lights out and bedtime at 9:00 pm.

It was during his first evening small group when Josh met Diana. She was a small girl from Williams County, VA in the western part of the state, out past Charlottesville. She had short brown hair, olive skin, and a dark freckle beside her nose.

For small group, boys and girls were mixed together.

There was no facilitator. The kids could talk about whatever they wanted, but they were encouraged to check in about how their days had gone.

"Today sucked," Diana said after the five of them— three boys and two girls—went around the circle they were sitting in and introduced themselves. "I'm stuck in this place where I can't listen to music, can't talk to friends, and can't watch TV. I don't get to wear shoes, makeup, regular clothes, or jewelry. When I'm not sharing my 'feelings' with somebody, I have to do schoolwork, while everybody here is trying to turn me into somebody I'm not. This is like the hell my parents told me I wouldn't have to go to until after I died."

Josh stared at Diana. He didn't mean to attract her attention, but his unblinking gaze drew her ire. With wide, angry eyes, Diana looked straight at him. "How was your day?" she asked. Her glare didn't give Josh a choice but to respond.

He cleared his throat. He said, "It was okay, I guess. I met my shrink, Dr. Powell—"

"She'll want you to call her Lorna," Diana interjected.

Josh said, "I told her I was a Satanist, and she took it all right."

At the word "Satanist," Diana's eyes lit up, which Josh noticed. But he didn't know what that meant. She could have been afraid, or she could have been intrigued. She asked, "What do you mean she took it all right?"

Josh looked back at Diana. He shrugged, "I mean, she didn't freak out or tell me I was wrong. She just listened."

"That's not fair," Diana said. "My doctor gets on my case every time I bring up Satan and what he means to me. But I'll tell you something," as if confiding a secret, Diana leaned closer to the group, "Lucifer's an angel. The people running this place, they're the devil."

Incredulity spread across Josh's face. The other three kids rolled their eyes and leaned away with awkward expressions.

Josh asked, "You're a Satanist?"

"What do you think I'm doing here?" Diana said. "My parents can't handle anything about me."

"Okay," one of the other guys interjected. He chuckled to break the tension. "I think that's enough about your crazy religion—"

"I don't think 'crazy' is a word you should use lightly around here," Diana said. She lifted one of her shoulders.

Josh was intrigued. As the other members of the group shared about their days, he was only thinking about Diana. He retreated back into himself for the rest of group.

As the week wore on, Josh tried finding every opportunity he could to learn more about Diana. Boys and girls didn't have too many opportunities to socialize in Safe Haven, but during each evening group, Josh tried talking to her a little more. He found out that where she grew up in Williams County, she was part of a coven that included her, a few teenage friends, and even some of her teachers at the local high school. That spun Josh for a loop. He lived alone with his practice. He conducted rituals in his attic, based loosely on the frameworks he'd learned from Anton LaVey's *Satanic Bible*, which he didn't even agree with.

Anton LaVey said Satan was a presence not a being. Josh believed in the being. He worshipped evil, which was the opposite of good. That's why he'd barely flinched when David had referred to himself as a Nazi. Whatever was good was bad. Whatever was bad was good.

Diana didn't like boys. "Unless you consider Lucifer a boy," she said. "Which some people might, but I think he's asexual. Because he's moved beyond our human concepts of pleasure."

Diana considered herself more a Luciferian than a Satanist. Although, she admitted Luciferianism was a kind of Satanism.

"But," she said, "Lucifer's the angel of light. He's not a dark presence. He's a force for knowledge and love. What most people consider God, that's the devil."

Josh listened. Although he disagreed. Diana's spirituality was as different from his as Anton LaVey's brand of atheistic Satanism was. But he was intrigued. He'd never known another person who claimed to be a Satanist. He wanted to believe he and Diana had more in common. He wanted to believe she might join his own nonexistent coven.

11.

"I've read your *Satanic Bible*." Annie Gladstone couldn't believe the words coming out of her mouth. Her son had only been in rehab for a week and a half. It was his second Tuesday there, the night of their first family therapy session together.

Annie's husband was sitting next to Annie on her right. Slouching down in his chair with a scowl on his face and a sneer on his lips, Josh was across from them.

With only socks on his feet, Josh wasn't dressed in his usual attire of a black heavy metal tee shirt. Along with music and Walkmans, band paraphernalia was outlawed in Safe Haven. Josh's mom had already dropped off a package of plain white undershirts. He was wearing one of them right then with skintight, acid-washed jeans. As he blew his hair out of his eyes, Josh looked like one of the greasers from the movie *The Outsiders*, the type of kid his dad had grown up with in Long Beach, CA, the type of kid an elementary school Josh had thought was the coolest.

Wayne, their family therapist, was sitting next to Annie and Bill, in between them and Josh. He'd introduced himself to Annie and Bill before a staff member brought Josh out to meet them. He told them not to expect much from the first few sessions. It might take their son a little while to come to terms with where he was and start working a treatment program. Wayne was still in his early thirties, making him younger than the two parents. But that didn't make a difference to Josh. He was still an adult. He had glasses and brown hair, and he took notes on a yellow pad of paper. The four of them were sitting in a small room with yellow cinder block walls.

The previous week, Annie had received a call from Josh's assigned psychiatrist—a woman with an accent that Annie couldn't place—informing her that her son claimed he worshipped the devil. He'd admitted to it in his first session. He had a copy of *The Satanic Bible* somewhere in his room, the woman told Annie. She suggested Annie find it and read it.

Annie discovered the book on the shelf beside Josh's bed. With the goat's head in the inverted pentacle on the black cover, she couldn't believe she'd never noticed it before. The author's photo on the back was such a terrifying attempt at evil it was comedic. Lit by a purple glare, a bald Anton Szandor LaVey stared down the camera with narrowed eyes above his black goatee.

With great trepidation, Annie read the book over the weekend. It wasn't as scary as she feared it might be, but it still wasn't a philosophy she wanted her son embracing. It was so selfish. Annie took notes on it so she could discuss it with Josh. She didn't believe in many of Anton LaVey's concepts, and she thought his refutation of religion was childish at best. Annie wasn't religious herself. She considered herself spiritual. She'd attended a Unity Church after Josh's father had left and before heading to Virginia with Bill, but Satanism was something she would never be able to relate to.

"You what?" Josh asked. Tomorrow would be his 15th birthday. He'd be locked up for it. Annie blinked. For a second, she thought the whole thing was a misunderstanding. It wasn't.

Annie said once again, "I've read your *Satanic Bible*." Repeating the words didn't help them make any more sense. She was talking to her son. The newborn she'd cradled against her chest as she recovered from her c-section in the hospital. The baby she'd nursed at her breast for the first eight months of his life. The child who'd worn a different hat to preschool every day as he played his games of make believe. She'd even helped the boy make a shadow box of a western-heading wagon train for his class project in second grade. This was Josh, her son. In an unconscious mimicry of his mother, Josh swallowed slowly.

He glared at Annie as if he hated her, which he believed he did. He wanted to spit on her—his desire to do so was overwhelming—but he didn't. He crossed his arms even tighter, and he slouched farther down in his chair. "Did you learn anything?" he asked.

"I did," Annie said. "I learned a lot."

Josh tilted his head to the side. He relaxed his shoulders. He looked at his mother as he had when he was a child and he didn't understand something she'd said.

At the sight of her son's visage, Annie's breath caught in her throat. Our personalities exist in our faces long before we grow into them. She said, "I learned that Satanists don't believe in God. They've chosen Satan as the opposite of Christianity, not as a deity to worship."

Josh nodded.

"So Satanists are really atheists. But they believe magic affects the world. So maybe they aren't atheists? I really don't understand what the author means by that."

Josh nodded again. "I don't agree with everything Anton LaVey says," he said.

Annie looked at her son. He didn't sound crazy. They might even be able to find some common ground. Even though Annie couldn't believe she was having this conversation with her 14-year-old child. It wasn't what she'd envisioned 13 years earlier when he'd been a toddler who'd laughed and squealed when she tickled his feet.

Josh said, "I believe there's a God, and I believe there's a devil. But I don't worship God. I worship the devil."

Annie's face drew down. That didn't make any sense. It made even less sense than Anton LaVey's *Satanic Bible*. Their conversation had taken a turn. Annie blinked. She asked, "So what you're saying is you believe in right and wrong, and you're choosing wrong? Why would you do that?"

Josh shrugged. "I don't have to tell you," he said.

Wayne cleared his throat. "Why won't you answer your mother?" he asked.

Josh looked at the therapist. His gaze was ice. "Because I don't like her," he said.

Wayne took Josh's comment in stride. "Just because you don't like somebody doesn't mean you shouldn't treat them with respect," he said. "She asked you a question."

"But I don't have to answer it, do I?"

"No. You don't have to answer it," Wayne said. He nodded. He looked down and wrote something on his notepad.

"What are you writing?" Josh demanded. Trying to see what Wayne had scratched onto his pad of paper, Josh leaned forward.

"I don't think I have to tell you that either," Wayne said, setting his pad aside.

"This is bullshit," Josh said. He crossed his arms and leaned back into his chair once again.

Annie started in place. "Josh," she said, "watch your language—"

"Or what, Mom? You'll lock me up? Too late. I'm stuck here until Wayne and the rest of these assholes say I can leave. I just want to move in with Dad."

"Your dad doesn't want you the way you are right now either," Annie said, but she immediately regretted how she'd phrased those words. Josh's countenance drew down.

"Well, screw him, then, too," Josh said.

"This isn't going anywhere," Bill Gladstone said.

"Where'd you expect it to go, Bill?" Josh asked. "You hit me."

Bill looked around as if he were lost. "Wait a second," he said. "You think I'd… I found him like that." He looked at Annie. He looked at Wayne. "I'd never hit him. He's my responsibility."

"Whatever, Bill," Josh said. "Keep saying that till somebody believes you." He looked away from everybody. His face was pretty much healed by then. There was still a scar above his lip, some discoloration around his eye. His mother frowned.

Josh said, "We all know you don't care about me. You just want my mom."

"That's not true," Bill said.

Annie looked from her son to her husband and back again. She said, "Josh, could you please show us all some respect? We've been trying to do that for you."

"Respect?" Josh said. His mouth moved in silence as he reached for his words. He said, "Locking me up and digging through my stuff is what you call respect?"

Annie looked down. "Maybe you're right. Maybe I

shouldn't have looked through your things."

"It's my house, Annie," Bill said. "And you're my wife. You can do what you want there."

"But it's my stuff," Josh said.

Annie hung her head. "He's right," she said. She sounded defeated. "It's his stuff."

"Who paid for it though?" Bill said. "You sure didn't." Above his mustache, he narrowed his eyes.

"It doesn't matter who paid for it," Annie said.

Trying to head off the impending argument now brewing between the parents, Wayne interjected, "I don't think this is getting us anywhere right now—"

"Nothing gets us anywhere," Josh said. He rolled his eyes, crossed his arms, and leaned back in his chair once again.

"What would get us somewhere then?" Wayne asked.

"Honesty," Josh said. He leaned forward in his chair. "A little honesty"

"Well, here's some honesty for you," Wayne said. "If you want to behave like an adult, you need to act like an adult and treat us as your equals rather than scowling and looking down on us all the time."

Josh huffed. "I don't want to be an 'adult,'" he said. "Not like you. Not like them. I just want to be left alone."

"You can't be," Annie said. "You're my son, and I love you."

Josh looked up at Annie. He tilted his head to the side. His gaze made it look like she was speaking a foreign language, but something registered behind Josh's eyes. It was as if those last words of his mother's had landed somewhere deeper than his mind. He pursed his lips and looked back down at the ground. "That doesn't mean anything," he said.

"I think it does," Wayne said.

"Love is bullshit," Josh said. "If it wasn't, I wouldn't be here."

12.

The next day, Josh didn't bother telling anybody it was his birthday. He was playing chess with David and moving his pieces lethargically. The other metalhead observed Josh's labored motions, but he didn't say anything. He didn't know what was bothering his new friend. Besides, he had a secret he wanted to share with Josh.

For his part, Josh was looking forward to small group that night. He wanted to see Diana again. He wanted to talk to her and hear more about her relationship with Lucifer. He wanted to tell her how poorly his parents, his psychologist, everybody understood him. Not even Carrie, his own girlfriend, had ever been able to reach through Josh's haze and touch his soul. Maybe Melody could. Maybe she already had. Josh didn't know. He sighed. He wanted to tell Diana it was his birthday. Maybe she'd say something to him that could help him celebrate.

David said, "I popped that dude in the face last night."

Josh looked up. David was glaring at somebody beyond Josh's shoulder. Josh turned slightly in his seat. In the distance, he saw Tyrell—the same black kid who'd slammed his fist into Josh and David's chess match the first morning Josh was there. Tyrell narrowed his eyes as

Josh turned around. He clenched his fists. He leaned over and whispered something to another black kid who was sitting next to him.

Across the table from Josh, David hissed, "What the hell, man? I didn't tell you to look."

Josh turned back around. He looked at David. His friend broke eye contact with the kid beyond Josh's shoulder. He looked back at their chess match. Josh cocked his head to the side. "I didn't see that," he said. He made his next move.

"Nobody saw," David said. Like a child sitting in his first preschool chair, he squirmed in his seat. He put his fingers on his queen, but he didn't move her. He said, "I waited till lights out. Then I snuck down the hallway to his room. I tapped him on the head so he woke up. So he knew who did it. And then I popped him right in the face. He started bawling like a baby. But I made it back to my room before any of the staff members got there. He won't be messing with us again." David moved his queen to take one of Josh's unguarded knights.

Josh frowned slightly. David figured it was because of the piece he'd lost. But in reality, Josh didn't think Tyrell had been messing with them at all. They'd had that argument during Josh's first day there, but Tyrell's reaction had made sense to Josh. David had offended him, and he'd responded. Ever since then, the black kid had kept his distance from the two metalheads.

Like David, Tyrell was non-CD. He claimed he'd been a drug dealer in the outside world, but he'd never used drugs. That's what he said at least. Tyrell and David had more interactions than he and Josh had. David and Tyrell were in the same group. They were in the same class at school. Tyrell didn't sit near them during any meals, and he didn't interact with them in the gym. He didn't really hang out with any of the other white kids in Safe Haven. Instead, he and the other black kid kept to themselves. The incident between the three of them had been over a week before. "I guess that's cool," Josh said. He wasn't even sure if the story David was telling was true.

"Of course, it's cool," David said. "Somebody needs to stand up to them, and who's going to do it besides us?" He smiled.

Josh gave a half-hearted smile in return. David assumed that was due to his friend's sour mood as well. But the truth was Josh wasn't sure if there was any reason to stand up to anybody who was stuck inside Safe Haven with them. And if there was, he certainly didn't think he was the one who needed to do it. He didn't have a problem with Tyrell. Whatever problem was brewing between David and him was solely of David's doing. Josh frowned. He shook his head and made his next move.

"All right," a staff member said over the noise of all the boys on the unit talking to one another at once, "time for small group."

Josh looked over his shoulder again. The girls were entering from their unit across the hall. The doors connecting the two units were usually locked. The only way to pass between them was with the help of a staff member. Josh kept staring at the girls until Diana walked through the door. They noticed one another and smiled.

The night before, during small group, Diana had revealed she was a vegetarian. "I refuse to eat anything that has feelings," she'd said.

Josh didn't understand. As a Satanist, he only wanted to eat things with feelings. Blood wasn't required, but it was always appreciated. Like the blood Josh had drawn from the cuts across his shoulders during his homespun rituals. He'd cut himself until a drop of blood flowed, and then he'd place it on a lone candle's flame. His scars remained. The whole world should suffer, Josh believed. But there was something about Diana's brand of Satanism that had Josh questioning his own. He didn't know what it was yet, but something was percolating at the edge of his thoughts. He broke eye contact with Diana and looked back at the game he was losing. He narrowed his gaze.

David appeared satisfied. "We can finish this later," he said in reference to their chess match, but Josh heard it as being in reference to their conversation. The game didn't have much longer to go, and not for the reasons David believed. Josh had finally noticed the next two moves he needed to make to capture the other metalhead's queen. After that, it was only a matter of time before he boxed in his king.

13.

The outdoor courtyard nestled inside Safe Haven's adolescent ward was dying. The trees were shedding their leaves. The grass was growing dormant. The brick walls surrounding the cold terrarium were faded and harsh. Even the windows looking in on the patients' rooms were dark and lifeless. In the mornings, frost clouded the glass. The stiff wind tickled Josh's cheeks as he walked circles out there beside his assigned psychiatrist, Dr. Lorna Powell.

The two of them traipsed across the concrete path along the courtyard's edge like old friends. Even though they'd only met the week before. Josh was wearing his shoes. It was the only time he'd be allowed to, when Lorna took him on a weekly walk outside Safe Haven's confines. Their hands were in their pockets. Their heads were bowed in concentration and conversation. When they spoke, mist pulsed from their lips. With concern creasing her features, the doctor listened carefully to what Josh had to say. Josh formed his words with precision. What he had to say mattered. His words meant something. It was only the second time he'd met with his doctor.

Unlike the other doctors at Safe Haven, Lorna insisted her patients call her by her first name rather than Dr.

Powell. She believed it made the adolescents she worked with more comfortable. That allowed them to open up more completely to her, and that allowed her to serve them better. Her goal wasn't to keep them in the hospital, collecting payment from their parents' insurance companies. Her goal was to set them free to live healthy lives outside those confines. The kids trusted Lorna. She was a person with a name. They were suspicious of doctors. Besides, harping on the rank and title—despite her hard work to achieve it—smelled of imperialism to Lorna. Having grown up black in Jamaica in the 1960s, that was a concept that never settled well with her.

"Tell me, then, why do you call yourself a Satanist?" Lorna asked Josh amid the natural ebb and flow of their conversation.

He'd been telling her how he wanted to be a rock star. He and Melody were going to run away to Los Angeles. Without judging, Lorna nodded and listened. The ease with which she'd posed her question had caught Josh off guard. He'd been telling her how much he cared for Melody. How Melody made him believe there might be something good in the world. When Lorna asked her question, Josh was willing to answer without hesitation. She wanted to know what he thought, and it felt to Josh like he might be able to convince her to see things his way.

Josh inhaled. As he exhaled, he narrowed his eyes. He said, "It's all just so empty."

Lorna narrowed her eyes as well. She looked at the windows and brick walls surrounding her and Josh. She tipped her head to the side. "What's so empty?" she asked.

"Everything. The whole world," Josh said.

Lorna's gaze opened up. "I think I understand," she said.

Josh looked at Lorna. He didn't say anything, but

something registered in his eyes too.

"You aren't the first person to think the world is empty, you know," Lorna said.

Josh frowned. He shrugged.

Lorna said, "There are thinkers you should read. You've read *The Satanic Bible*, but that's too simple for somebody like you. You need to read authors like Franz Kafka and Albert Camus. They say and think things very similar to what you do, but they don't need a justification for their beliefs. You should read them when you get out of here. You might like them. You might relate to them, and you might find they become your friends."

Josh was already reading a lot in Safe Haven. He'd found a copy of *The Diary of Anne Frank* in one of his classrooms. David had asked him why he was bothering to read something by a dead Jew. He thought Josh's psychiatrist was starting to rub off on him, but Josh didn't care what David thought. Josh's mother was Jewish. David didn't know that.

Anne Frank was Josh's same age. She was like the girls he knew—Melody, Carrie, and Tina. She cared about boys. She cared what boys thought about her. She kept a diary. It was beautiful. But there was no end to it. It simply stopped one day.

After he finished that book, Josh started reading another book he'd found in his classroom at Safe Haven called *On the Beach*. It took place in Australia after a nuclear war. A radiation cloud was coming for the inhabitants. Everybody was waiting to die. It was only a matter of time.

Josh remembered lying in bed when he'd been younger, before the Berlin Wall had fallen, when everybody believed the United States and the Soviet Union were going to go to war. He remembered being terrified of seeing a flash of light on the horizon, a mushroom cloud puffing up in the direction of downtown Los Angeles, and realizing he was going to die soon. It wasn't going to happen in some distant time and place. It was happening right then. Josh wondered what it would be like. Would there be something? Would there be nothing? In Safe Haven, that thought reminded him of sitting on the floor in his den upstairs one afternoon, listening to music and trying to write a poem. Then Josh realized that even if there never was a nuclear war, everybody was still waiting to die. It was only a matter of time. That made Josh sad. For himself. For everybody.

One night, as Josh was drifting off to sleep, he thought about when he'd made the decision to sell his soul. He'd been in sixth grade. He'd been hurt by his parents' divorce, his grandfather's death, and his move across the country. He'd been angry, but he hadn't always been so angry. When he'd been a kid, when his parents had lived together and his grandfather had been in his life, he'd been a happy child. For three and a half years, that happiness had rotted in his gut. He couldn't digest the past.

Staring at the shadows crisscrossing the ceiling above him, Josh was lying on his back in his bed. His hands were clasped behind his neck. His roommate was mumbling in his sleep in the bed on the other side of the tiny room they shared. Josh wanted to go to sleep too, but something wasn't settling right with him. He narrowed his eyes and stared closer at the shadows on the ceiling.

He remembered when he'd made the decision to worship the devil. He'd been on a plane back to California to visit his dad. His grandfather was dead. He was listening to a tape on his Walkman. The band was shouting at the devil, and that got Josh thinking. Nobody loved him. He knew that. If they did, they wouldn't treat him the way they did. But God was loved by everybody. Josh didn't want to worship a being that already felt the world's love. Josh was more akin to the creature the world hated— Satan.

In his room in Safe Haven, Josh's thoughts turned to *The Diary of Anne Frank*, and David's Nazism felt like a swarm of flies buzzing around his head. The insects wormed their way into Josh's mind. Paper wings and antenna flew across his mouth and lungs. They were suffocating him. They were hatred, pure hatred, the nuclear explosion on the horizon that was coming to destroy his world.

All Josh had wanted to do was rebel. That's what had led him to heavy metal and Satan. He'd wanted a better world than the one his parents had given him. But Josh wasn't building a better world. He was always wasted. David's racism inundated him. Carrie probably wouldn't have been hooking up with him if her older brother had never done to her what he'd done to her. Josh wasn't helping anybody. He was hurting everybody. He remembered what that preppy kid, Matt, had said at that AA meeting a few weeks before. He'd said he was *sick and tired of being sick and tired.* Josh knew then what Matt had been talking about. Something had to change. Josh knew it.

A vision of a video he'd seen on MTV came back to Josh. Black men had been dressed in military uniforms. One guy wore a clock around his neck because time meant something, but Josh didn't know what it was. The video was for the song *Welcome to the Terrordome* by the rap group Public Enemy. As they'd sat in Todd's mom's apartment after school that day, Josh's friend had made fun of it. He'd used derogatory names for the members of the group. But Josh had listened to the song. He'd listened to what the lead rapper, Chuck D, had to say. He couldn't remember any of the words the rapper had used, but he remembered how the rhymes had made him feel.

As he lay in bed in that hospital room in Safe Haven, Josh realized Public Enemy was the real rebellion. Josh had been misled. There was a deeper rebellion than the one he'd embarked upon. For a second before he closed his eyes, Josh knew that. As he drifted off to sleep that night, he knew when he awoke the following morning, things would be very different for him.

14.

Diana always signed her notes to Josh: *Remember, Satan loves you.* That baffled him. He worshipped Satan because he believed the devil had nothing to do with love. Josh had seen the kind of damage that emotion could cause. He'd felt its pain firsthand. He'd suffered through it when his parents had split up. It had ripped his soul apart when his grandfather had died. It had punched him in the gut when he'd moved to Virginia and tried to build relationships with his new classmates. Nothing ever worked out.

Josh still remembered his first year in Virginia. It had been even worse than his last year in California. He'd never been a popular kid in elementary school, but he'd had friends of a sort. After his parents split up the summer before fourth grade, however, Josh had a hard time relating to his peers any longer. Minor slights became unforgivable affronts. By the time he got to Virginia in sixth grade, Josh couldn't handle the kind of hazing his classmates visited upon him. He reacted sharply and definitively. First, by crying himself to sleep at night. Later, by responding with violence and visions of insanity. He wanted to do drugs so his peers could see there was nothing he wouldn't do to destroy himself. He wanted them to know he worshipped the devil so they might imagine what he would do to them if they crossed him one more time.

With a grin, Diana handed her notes off to Josh at night during their small group sessions. Josh read them when he got back to his room, before he went to bed. Since the notes were contraband, he didn't save them. He slept with them under his pillow, and he threw them away in the cafeteria every morning at breakfast. But he enjoyed receiving them.

In her notes, Diana talked about her life back in Williams County. She described her coven. They all dressed in black. Their English teacher was the High Priest. She couldn't tell Josh about the rituals. They were secret. But she invited him to join them someday as an initiate. The proposition both excited and frightened Josh. He'd always performed his rituals alone. He'd told Diana he was his own coven's High Priest. But that was only because he was the only one in his coven. Diana didn't know that.

It was pleasant to have a connection inside Safe Haven. Josh didn't know if Diana was interested in him—she'd said she didn't like boys. And Josh didn't know if he was interested in her in that way either. He had a girlfriend back home, or at least, when he'd gotten locked up he'd had a girlfriend back home. He didn't know if that was still the case. Marcus probably still blamed him for everything that had been going on the day he went over there with Todd. And the girl had no idea where Josh was and why he hadn't been able to at least try and reach out to her. So he appreciated his connection with Diana.

Everything else was so lifeless. Especially after his birthday. The walls of Safe Haven were cold. The world outside was dying. The inmates were drugged. Even the institution's artwork was uninspired. It hung on the walls like cotton candy. At least Diana, and her relationship with Lucifer, felt alive. Her notes reached out to Josh as if they were springtime rejuvenating the world. He didn't know what to make of the sensation.

David was another story entirely. Just like with Diana, Josh didn't know what to do about his fellow metalhead. But for entirely different reasons. Where Diana lightened Josh's load, David contributed to it. Where Diana brought pleasure, David brought suffering. And the most disturbing thing to Josh about it all was—with their shared anger—David and he had even more in common than he had with Diana. Diana's Lucifer was love. Like Josh's Satan, David's Nazism was pure hate. It turned Josh's stomach. It brought a frown to his lips when David smiled at him during their chess matches. It was as if David could sense their spiritual proximity. Of course, David assumed his new friend didn't like the circumstances under which they'd met, but the truth was Josh didn't want them to be friends at all. He didn't want them to have anything in common.

The two of them—Diana and David—formed a duality defining Josh's experience in Safe Haven. It wasn't a duality Josh had ever intended to confront, but it existed. He didn't know what it meant. But it referenced two directions his present circumstances could diverge into. Josh needed a third way. He'd never understood there was more than one form that evil could take. He'd thought his devil was the only one. He'd forgotten the lesson he'd learned when watching *The Exorcist 3* in a darkened movie theatre with Melody the year before: *The devil is many; God is One.* But even if he'd remembered that, he couldn't have known what it meant.

As they did every night, David and Josh were playing

chess when the girls entered the boy's unit for small group. Josh had just captured one of David's knights when he heard the door between their two sides click. A staff member unlocked the door. With a rush of female voices, the door swung open. Josh turned in his chair to see the girls walk in. He wasn't aware of it, but what he really wanted was to make eye contact with Diana. He held his breath as he waited for her to appear.

David was going to be leaving Safe Haven the following morning. His excitement was revealed by his mannerisms. There was a flippancy to how he moved his chess pieces that evening. He spoke with a playfulness he didn't usually possess. It annoyed Josh. Not because the other headbanger wanted to leave as well, but simply because he couldn't stand David any longer. He was ready for his so-called friend to be gone. He had things he needed to think about. Decisions needed to be made. He'd been discussing it all with Lorna, his psychiatrist. David—and his beliefs—was a distraction.

Josh still had another five days left before the end of his 30-day program. Thirty days was the longest his parents' insurance company would allow him to stay, and Lorna had promised his parents she'd have him released before anybody had to pay out of pocket. Josh didn't mind the wait though. He still wasn't thrilled with his mother's decision to put him away, but he was beginning to believe his life might need to change. Maybe he wouldn't get back in touch with Todd on the day he left Safe Haven. Maybe the two of them needed some distance from each other. Maybe it was even for the best if Marcus didn't want him around Carrie anymore. She certainly didn't need somebody like him in her life. She had enough problems of her own without worrying about Josh compounding them. He was starting to think he may not run away to

Los Angeles when he turned 16 either. That was the first time in nearly four years he'd considered that. He even wondered how Melody would feel if he got clean. He believed she'd still accept him, but he didn't know. That was the thought that made him the most nervous.

Diana entered the boy's unit. As usual, when she scanned the room, her eyes met Josh's. She smiled and looked away. Josh wanted to wave, but he also didn't want to draw attention to their relationship. He looked down. Diana fidgeted with the tight fabric on the legs of her jeans. Subtle emotions warmed Josh's stomach. He looked forward to whatever Diana's note to him that night might say.

David snickered. "Your dyke girlfriend just showed up," he said.

Josh's head snapped up. He looked at David, and he tilted his head to the side, "What did you say?"

"Nothing." David was still smiling. "I just don't know why you'd want to bang a chick who only wants to bang other chicks."

With the alacrity of a cat, Josh sprang out of his chair and across the table—scattering chess pieces over the floor just as Tyrell had done on Josh's first morning there—to grab David by the throat. They both tumbled backward out of David's chair. David's head slammed into the thin carpet. With a grunt, Josh landed on top of him. Josh brought his arm back. Before David could maneuver his hands up to block, Josh slammed his fist into David's face once… twice. A splash of blood sprayed out of David's nose and across Josh's knuckles.

David slithered out from underneath Josh. Josh reached for him with all the rage that had built over their three weeks locked up together. Powerful arms grabbed Josh from behind. They wrestled him into a full nelson hold. Josh was staring at the floor. He blew his hair out of his face and tried looking up. David wiped the blood from his nose. A splash of blood was painted across his tee shirt as well.

"Easy there, killer," a staff member said from behind Josh. Josh struggled to extricate himself from the staff member's embrace, but that only brought the hold together stronger.

"What was that for?" David asked. He was still holding his nose. His voice sounded nasally.

Josh heaved for breath. Adrenalin coursed through his limbs. "Everything," he said.

The staff member spun Josh around. He noticed Tyrell smiling in the corner. The staff member forced Josh back to his bedroom. He would be put in gowns. He'd spend his last five days in Safe Haven unable to leave the boy's side of the unit. He wouldn't attend small group at night with Diana anymore. He wouldn't get any more letters from her. She wound up leaving two days later. She was going to tell him that in the letter she'd written him that night, but Josh never got a chance to receive it. Before David left the following morning, Josh didn't say another word to him. The two of them never spoke again, and Josh was fine with that.

III.

15.

In the distance, the cloudless California sky merged with the Pacific Ocean. The two elements of air and water blended together. They melded into a third element, something like ether. From where he sat cross-legged on the beach, one hand enmeshed within the sand surrounding him, Josh took a drag off his cigarette. He exhaled. Smoke drifted over his right shoulder and up to where the sun warmed his back. Death moved closer. Josh felt it catch in his lungs. He was always afraid of cancer. It would be ironic for him to have lived through everything he had only to succumb to lung cancer in his first year of sobriety at just 15 years old. But he was only scared for a second. His mind and the rest of his body still felt as alive as when he'd left rehab eight months earlier. He breathed easier.

Josh was sitting on the beach in a pair of black, knee-length board shorts. It had been eight months since he'd gotten out of Safe Haven, even longer since he'd last seen Carrie Condrey and his once-upon-a-time best friend, Todd Campbell, who had had to move back in with his father down on the Petersburg Pike. The two of them hadn't seen each other since the night Josh had gotten locked up.

Saltwater dripped off Josh's arms and chest. It pelted the hot sand. He wiped a drop running from his nose. Stuck into the sand beside him, his surfboard rose up to cast its long, diamond shadow beside him. His dad had bought that board for him when he'd first shown up in California that summer. It glistened with surf wax and saltwater.

Josh hadn't been surfing long. He'd learned from Matt, that preppy kid he'd met at the AA meeting, only two and a half months earlier, but from the moment he'd first felt a board glide across the ocean, when he'd first seen the sheen of salt water slip across its surface, he'd fallen in love in a way that he'd only ever loved music before.

On a beach in North Carolina, Matt had placed a surfboard deck-side up on the sand. He lay down and slid up his arms to push his chest off until he could hop up on his legs and stand hunched over the board. Then he asked Josh if he wanted to try. Josh jumped up and lay back down about twenty times before Matt told him they should paddle out into the ocean. Josh didn't think he was ready yet. But Matt smiled and said, "You can't learn how to do it until you do it."

Unlike Matt, Josh had never skated when he was younger. Riding a wave didn't come naturally to him. But he'd spent his summers in Southern California body surfing with his dad. He knew how to catch a wave. Poking white fingers into the air, the wave's face frothed at its tips. It was just starting to break. Josh paddled and kicked. Before he knew it, he was caught up in the surge. He pushed down on his board and slid up to stand. But his balance was off. The board tipped to the left. Josh tumbled into the water. After splashing around in the shore break for a few seconds, Josh grabbed hold of his ankle leash. He pulled himself back to his board and paddled out to meet up with Matt again.

"Nice work, man," Matt said. He was sitting on his own board in the middle of the ocean, flexing his arms and chest as water dripped off his wiry muscles. "Try standing up on the next one though," he said. He smiled.

Josh smiled back. When he'd gotten out of Safe Haven in November and started attending AA meetings in earnest, he and Matt quickly became friends. That conversation they'd shared together in the graveyard the week before Josh had gotten locked up had precipitated their bond. They'd wound up sharing a great deal about their lives with each other that night. Smoking cigarettes until Josh's mom had shown up, they'd discussed their histories with drugs and alcohol and their feelings about their parents and their respective divorces. They'd talked about music and movies. They'd even discussed their current girlfriends. Matt was dating the blond girl from the meeting who looked like Melody but with straight hair. It had been as if the half hour they'd spent waiting for Josh's mom had somehow extended into a peaceful eternity.

The first thing Josh asked his mom to do for him when he got out of Safe Haven was to take him to get his haircut. He got it cut evenly one length all the way around. It hung right below his eyes in the front, halfway over his ears on the sides, and to the top of his neck in the back. He also got it shaved underneath. It was a longer version of the same haircut many of his peers were already wearing. He bought a new pair of white low-top Chuck Taylor's, a relatively generic type of shoe that was unlike the metalhead style of black high-top Reeboks he'd worn for the past three years. He also bought new shirts and pants. The clothes were all a looser fit than the skintight shirts and jeans all the headbangers wore. He didn't want anything with a visible label on it either, nothing that would confine him to a clique or personality. He didn't want to be a metalhead, a skater, a prep, or a jock.

When Josh got back from the mall with his mom, Bill was eating lunch in the kitchen. He'd been at work when the two of them had left that morning. Between bites off his bologna sandwich, Bill smiled at Josh's new haircut and clothes. His eyes teared up. Wiping his mouth with a paper napkin, he walked over and gave his stepson a hug. Even though he didn't feel any better about Bill's presence in his life, the man's reaction made Josh proud. He smiled back at his stepdad, and he went upstairs to listen to his new CD—Jane's Addiction's *Ritual de lo habitual.*

From the opening words of that album's first track to the closing notes of the album's final song, Josh was enthralled. The song *Three Days'* complexity opened up a world of emotions in Josh that he'd never known he could feel. As the tune built from a reflective acoustic piece into the album's heaviest piece, Josh tried figuring out what Jane's Addiction's singer, Perry Farrell, was talking about in the lyrics. The song was rife with imagery and symbolism.

The words reminded Josh of the album's red cover with the naked man and woman cuddling up to the third woman between them. Josh thought of when he'd lain down on his carpet while he was tripping and listened to The Doors only a couple months before. He'd been writing that poem for English class. He'd grown afraid of God and the devil. Sober, he wasn't afraid anymore. Josh felt a lightness in his stomach. He understood what his dad had always told him about poetry and music, how words could mean something and move you more so even than the music alone. One of those cryptic answers his dad always gave him on their weekly calls finally fell into place in Josh's soul.

It was only a few months after that when Josh's mom told Bill he had to leave. An anonymous package had been dropped off at their door one morning. In the package was a videotape of Bill having an affair with another woman. Annie knew the woman. She was a mutual friend of theirs who they'd met when Annie and Bill first moved to Potterfield County.

Bill denied it, but Annie had proof. She told her husband to get out of their home immediately. He agreed, but he wasn't happy about it.

Two days later—while he was watching the Rodney King protests on CNN—Josh got a call from Bill's business partner, a man named Denny McHugh. Denny was in Alcoholics Anonymous as well. As the main investor in Bill's company, he was the reason Annie, Bill, and Josh had moved to Potterfield County in the first place.

Denny was a tall, lanky man with gray hair. In his early 50s with a concealed carry permit, he kept a handgun strapped to his ankle. He was the first person who'd ever suggested to Annie that she might try bringing her son to an AA meeting. That day, though, in April 1992 when Denny called Josh, he was calling to tell the teenager he needed to get out of the house right then. Bill had just left the office. He was rushing home to get something he kept hidden there before Annie got back from her first meeting with a lawyer. It would probably be best if Josh weren't around when Bill arrived.

As soon as he hung up, Josh snuck out the house and ran through the woods the same way he always had when he'd been using drugs and alcohol. Running and panting, he swatted the hanging branches out of his face. One scratched him below the eye. He knew the paths to avoid the road. When he'd been drinking, he'd learned them so he wouldn't have any run-ins with the cops. There was a curfew for kids under 16 in Potterfield County. Five months sober, Josh was grateful he could evade his stepdad. As horribly as they'd gotten along when Bill was living with them, Josh had no idea how the man might treat him now that he was accused of having an affair. He could still remember Bill's enraged face inches from his own that night he'd had his last drink.

Josh met up with Denny a couple miles from his home. He hopped in the older man's BMW, and he spent the rest of the afternoon at Denny's tract mansion in an even wealthier Louthain neighborhood.

At Denny's place, Josh was reclining on a leather couch in the man's library perusing a copy of the *Bhagavad-Gita*. Josh had never come across the book before, but it looked interesting. A thin work, the frame story of the Kurukshetra War first caught Josh's attention. He was struck by how Arjuna was being asked to kill his own family members. That sounded difficult and far from what Josh would have assumed to be righteous. He would have thought saving lives rather than taking lives was what the Godhead would require. But what most enthralled the newly sober Josh was Krishna's exhortation to Arjuna's sense of duty. Josh set the book aside and pondered what his own duty might be.

"Interesting choice," Denny said. He was standing in the doorway, leaning against the doorframe. "I thought you would have gone in for Burroughs or Kerouac. Spiritualism isn't in most teens' wheelhouse."

Josh looked back at Denny's bookshelf. He shrugged.

He thought of when he'd first gotten out of Safe Haven. He'd come home from school one day. His mom was out, and Bill was still at work. Josh felt a presence in their house. It constricted his throat and tightened his stomach. Josh was afraid. A dark figure haunted him. He thought back to the rituals he'd conducted in the attic upstairs. He'd light a candle atop the trunk where he kept his empty liquor bottles. He'd cast a circle, point a knife to the four winds, and call on demonic forces to offer him assistance.

Those forces were no longer contained within the circle however. They floated freely through Josh's home. Instead of trembling in fear though Josh fell on his knees in the foyer. He rested his hands and chin upon the chair his mom had been sitting in when Mr. Fisher dropped him off that morning after he and Todd had slept in the woods, his grandfather's chair. Josh envisioned a golden light encircling him. He prayed to St. Michael to cleanse his house from the presences he'd unleashed.

With a flash of blue light, the angel flew down from the heavens with a fiery sword and battled the demonic presences haunting Josh there on the earthly plane. When the battle was won, Josh crossed himself as a Catholic would. He kissed his fingers and held them aloft to the sky. Still envisioning St. Michael standing over his shoulder, he stood up and strode boldly through the house.

Denny said, "You need a teacher, Josh, a 'spiritual advisor' as they used to say in AA when I was a newcomer. I could be that for you."

"Sure," Josh said. On some level, he agreed with the man. A powerful spiritual presence welled inside him. It overflowed from his core to his limbs. But it died at the extremities of his physical being. He needed guidance to learn how to channel and control it. He needed guidance to face whatever trials might come.

Denny smiled. As if quoting scripture, he looked up. He said, "When the teacher is ready, the student will appear."

One of the first suggestions Denny made as Josh's spiritual advisor was that Josh join him and the other young people from Louthain's AA meetings at one of Denny's two beach houses in North Carolina. Acquiescing to his advisor's influence, Josh agreed. That was where Matt taught Josh how to surf.

16.

Josh rode down to the beach with Denny and Pete, the lanky kid from Louthain's AA meetings. Only a year older than Josh, Pete was easily as tall as Josh's dad. But whereas Josh's dad still carried the build that had allowed him to play college football, Pete was built more like Joey Ramone, the singer for the punk band the Ramones. In fact, with his black hair and bony features, he might have even resembled the Ramones' lead singer if his hair were long rather than short. Of course, Pete's clothing was also more in line with the hip hop style most of the kids in Potterfield's AA circles were wearing rather than the Ramones' classic rocker look. In a pair of baggy jeans and a loose-fitting tennis shirt, he was dressed like one of Carrie's brothers.

Up front, Denny and Pete were talking about April, the girl at the AA meetings who looked like Melody and was dating Josh's new friend, Matt.

"She's just so hot," Pete said. He laughed at his admission. Denny agreed, which rubbed Josh the wrong way. Denny was far too old to think a girl Josh's age was hot. The comment reminded Josh of Bill, his soon-to-be ex-stepdad. But since Pete kept right on smiling at the man, Josh assumed Denny's assessment must have been okay with his new friend, and he forgot his discomfort.

"You got a girlfriend?" Pete asked. Draping one arm over the headrest, he turned around in his seat and stared at Josh.

"No," Josh said. He frowned and shook his head.

Josh had tried calling Carrie when he'd gotten out of Safe Haven. Her mom had answered the phone.

"Carrie's not allowed to talk to you anymore," her mother said, and she hung up the phone.

Josh understood. He hung up the phone too. He hadn't expected to continue dating Carrie. He'd simply never said goodbye. He'd been gone for a month, but he still wanted to apologize to her. He'd never treated her fairly. Even though he wanted to get clean, a pit opened in his gut. There were so many things he'd realized while he was in Safe Haven that he wanted to say to her.

Two days later, Carrie called him back. Her mom and brothers were out. But she didn't know how long they'd be gone. Josh needed to say what he had to say fast.

"I wanted to apologize," Josh said.

"For what?" Carrie asked.

"For everything," Josh said.

There was silence on the other end of the line. Then Carrie said, "I told my mom about Isaac. Just like you told me to."

Josh swallowed slowly. "What did she say?"

"Just that she wished I'd told her earlier. That's it. There's nothing she can do."

Josh sighed. "I'm sorry," he said.

"Anyway," Carrie said. "I can't talk to you anymore."

"I know," Josh said.

"I started dating somebody new."

"I figured," Josh said.

That conversation had happened four months earlier. Josh didn't know it at the time, but that was the last time he would ever get a call from Carrie Condrey. It was for the best. In Denny's car on the way down to North Carolina, Pete turned back around to look out the front windshield once again. "Yeah, Matt's one hell of a lucky guy," he said.

Josh smiled at his own reflection. It gazed back at him from the window overtop the cars cruising along beside them. He looked so different than he remembered himself looking. His haircut added a layer of youth to the shape of his face. His eyes no longer carried a constant rage. He felt at peace.

"Did you listen to those tapes I gave you?" Denny asked from up front.

Josh glanced up. From behind his sunglasses, Denny was staring back at Josh in the rearview mirror. He should have kept his eyes on the road. Josh said, "Yeah. I started to."

"What did you think?" Denny asked.

"They're cool," Josh said.

A few weeks earlier, Denny—as Josh's spiritual advisor—had given Josh some meditation tapes. The purpose of the tapes was to induce an out of body experience. Josh had listened to them. After he got home from school, he lay down on his bed with earphones on. He closed his eyes, and he pressed play on his Walkman. A soothing voice helped him relax. Electronic music tingled across his eardrums. But the desired out of body experience never materialized. Josh fell asleep. He'd expected it. As badly as he wanted to believe, he simply didn't think out of body experiences were real.

"Did they work?" Denny asked. A certain longing

persisted in his voice.

"Not yet," Josh said. He wanted to add something to show his faith in the process, but he couldn't think of anything more to say. He bit his lip.

"Just give it time. They'll—" Denny swerved the wheel. At over 80 mph, their car crossed into the next lane.

"What was that!" Pete shouted.

Josh's heart was pounding. He never heard the sound of tearing, crashing metal that he expected to hear. He touched his chest to make sure he was still alive. He was. They were okay. He breathed a little easier.

"That Nissan came from out of nowhere," Denny said.

Pete laughed. "He scared the hell out of me," he said.

"He did, huh?" Denny said. "Well, we'll give him something to be afraid of." Denny reached down beside the door. The sound of ripping Velcro filled the car. Soon Denny was holding a Colt .38 Special aloft in his right hand. Denny's palm closed around the pistol grip. His finger sat beside the trigger. He pressed the accelerator.

Josh slunk down in his seat, but he kept looking out the window nonetheless. As they passed the silver Nissan on its right, Denny looked to his left. The driver glanced over as well. From his shocked expression, Josh could tell the driver saw Denny brandishing his .38.

17.

Pete laughed as he told Matt and Matt's little brother, Mikey, the story of Denny flaunting his weapon at that driver in the Nissan. "I swear to God, he slammed on his brakes and just let us cruise on by," Pete said.

Mikey chuckled with a staccato laugh. But Matt appeared concerned. He made eye contact with Josh who shrugged and looked away. Mikey and Matt had driven down to North Carolina together in Matt's car. They'd left Louthain a little later than Denny, Pete, and Josh. Matt had had class that afternoon at the local community college. At 17 years old, he was the youngest student in his class, but he already had his GED.

Mikey might have been Matt's younger brother, but he was still almost a year older than Josh. There were only 17 months separating the two brothers. And even though he was old enough, he didn't have his driver's license yet. He was taking his time. He wanted to stay a kid for a little while longer. There was no reason to grow up so fast.

Pete didn't have his driver's license yet either. Even though he too was a year older than Josh. But Pete's reason was entirely different. He'd been arrested for marijuana at 15. And in the Commonwealth of Virginia, if you'd been arrested as a minor for drugs, your license was suspended until you turned 17. It didn't matter that Pete had lived in Arizona when he'd been arrested. The law still applied.

"Let's go see what the girls are up to," Pete said. He smiled. The girls had come down with Pete's legal guardian, a woman named Laurie. They were staying at Denny's other beach house. Laurie had known Pete when he was a child in Tucson, AZ. She'd dated his father who was an alcoholic as well, just like Pete's mother. When Pete got arrested at 15, Laurie had offered to take him in and give him a fresh start. So far, that fresh start had worked out well for Pete. He'd been sober since he'd first moved to Virginia, and he had friends, something which had been sorely lacking from his life in Tucson.

As the boys approached, all three girls were sitting out on the back balcony of Denny's condo. As they trudged up the sandy beach, the four boys could hear the girls laughing. From a black boombox, the girls were blasting the newest Red Hot Chili Peppers' CD, *Blood Sugar Sex Magik*. Even though the album had been out for more than six months, Josh hadn't heard it yet. He wasn't a fan of the band.

Melody had started listening to the Red Hot Chili Peppers at the end of eighth grade. Josh remembered seeing the tape cover for their previous album, *Mother's Milk*, one day when he'd been over at her mom's apartment that past summer. In miniature, the four band members had been cupped in a woman's arms, looking up at her face over her bare breast. Over the summer, Melody hadn't played the tape for Josh. Of course, she'd assumed her friend wouldn't be into it. Even though she was.

Back then Josh had been surprised. He didn't think his friend would listen to that sort of stuff. The Chili Peppers seemed so different. They had a sense of humor, which most metal didn't have. Humor was punk's domain. Metal was sincere with its anger. But now Josh was willing to give the band a chance. Along with Jane's Addiction and Public Enemy, their funk-inspired sound seemed like the kind of music he might be listening to going forward.

"Their singer is sober, you know," Pete said.

As he struggled up the sand dunes in his white Chuck Taylor's, Josh looked askance at his new friend.

"It's true," Pete said. He nodded. Breathing heavily as he stumbled through the sand in his own shoes, he slipped but quickly caught himself. "One of their songs is even about getting clean from heroin."

Josh didn't know which song that might be. He didn't listen to the radio, and he didn't watch MTV anymore. He sat alone in his room, going through the music he'd always loved, trying to figure out who he still wanted to listen to. Other than some punk bands, the only bands who had made the cut were Anthrax and Suicidal Tendencies. Neither of them dealt with Satan, and they both came off as concerned about themselves and their world.

"Well, just because he's clean doesn't mean he's sober," Matt said. He didn't look up as he spoke. But it didn't matter. Nobody could see his eyes behind his white-framed sunglasses. He wasn't wearing shoes. Instead, he was carrying a pair of flip-flops in his hand.

Pete shrugged. He mumbled, "I think he's sober."

"Hey!" April shouted from above as she and the other two girls noticed the boys.

The four boys looked up as one. Matt smiled at April. Josh locked eyes with Melody. Mikey grinned. The third girl, Sian, gazed down at Josh who she'd never met. Pete wanted to shield his eyes against all three girls' beauties ringed by the setting sun. He was smitten with each of them. Even though he didn't believe he stood a chance with any of them.

Sian lived in Heimrich, the county west of Richmond. The other kids on that trip were all from south of the city. And while both Melody and April dyed their hair blond. Sian's was a natural brown. Melody knew her through her new boyfriend.

While Josh was locked up in Safe Haven, Melody had started dating a guy who was clean and sober as well. By the time Josh got out of the hospital, Melody already had almost thirty days clean. She was extremely supportive of her best friend embarking on a new way of life.

Aaron, Melody's new boyfriend, had adopted Josh into his circle, but Josh hadn't hit it off with him the way he did with Matt. Aaron went to a different 12-step program than Matt did. He still had long hair. He drove a pick-up truck, and he loved Metallica's most recent, self-titled album. He was more or less a metalhead who didn't drink. Josh wanted to get as far away from his old way of life as he could.

Matt and April had met Sian during their travels to other meetings around Richmond. Pete had bumped into her once with Matt and April. And Mikey knew her through his brother as well. Of course while all seven kids were sober, only the six southsiders went to the same meetings together each week. But Sian wasn't an outcast. She'd ingratiated herself with the other two girls, and Melody was excited to introduce her to her best friend, Josh.

That night, Sian and Josh were sitting atop a wooden lifeguard tower on the beach looking out at the dark sky bending into the black ocean. The dunes were behind them. Probably to make out in private, Matt and April had disappeared beneath the pier a few yards away. At the bottom of the lifeguard tower, Mikey and Pete were talking with Melody about music.

The two boys were showing off in their own, individual ways. Mikey was smiling and cracking jokes. Pete was bringing gravity to the conversation. Of course Melody held up her end fine, which impressed the boys. Even though she was secretly thrilled about Sian and Josh being alone together atop the tower. Neither of them had been involved with anybody since they'd gotten sober. For Josh, that was almost six months ago. For Sian, it had been eight.

But romance didn't seem to be on Josh's mind. Even if it was on Sian's. Atop the lifeguard tower, Josh said, "There are just so many things I need to make up for. I don't know how I'll ever be able to do it." The wind carried his voice away. It disappeared in the night. As if there were spirits listening in the darkness, Josh stared into the distance.

Sian followed Josh's gaze, but she didn't see anything there. She looked back carefully at Josh's face. "We've all made mistakes," she said. Josh appeared so sincere. Sian's eyes creased. "Especially when we were using—"

"But it wasn't just the things I did." Josh inhaled. "Those kinds of things you can make amends for." He said, "It was the things I thought and said, the energies I brought into this world."

"But you can make amends for that too." Sian leaned down to catch Josh's eye. He looked at her. She smiled. "Just bring a different energy with you."

Two and a half months later, as Josh was sitting on the beach in Southern California, staring at the early evening sky meeting a different ocean—but there's really only one ocean, he thought about what Sian had said in the humid North Carolina night once again. She was right. He needed to figure out how to bring a new kind of energy into the world. He put his cigarette out in the sand, and he looked back over his shoulder. Walking barefoot across the beach as if he'd been walking on sand since the beginning of time, Josh's dad was making his way toward him. Josh inhaled deeply. The whole world smelled of the ocean's salt. It was time to go.

18.

Since April rode back with Matt and Mikey and since Denny and Pete were staying an extra day, Josh rode back from his first beach trip with Melody, Sian, and Pete's guardian, Laurie. Melody had first suggested the idea that same morning. Josh accepted because he assumed Melody wanted him to ride with her. In reality, however, she was hopeful about how much time Sian and Josh had spent together over the weekend. She thought the long ride back to Richmond would cement their friendship. It might even start them down the road to something more.

The night before, as they were falling asleep in the bed they were sharing in Denny's condo, Melody had asked Sian what she thought of Josh.

"He's cute," Sian said above the waves crashing against the shore outside. As if she were still trying to find her balance in the ocean, she could feel them tugging and pushing at her legs. "And he seems really sweet."

"He is really sweet," Melody said. She smiled. Sian could hear the positivity radiating through her new friend's voice. Josh had problems. He always had. But to Melody, he'd always been kind. She knew his soul. If he allowed it, it could fly free on golden wings.

"Why aren't you two dating?" Sian asked. She inhaled

deeply. The smell of saltwater still permeated her world. She stared at the shadows spreading across the ceiling.

Melody shrugged. She frowned, but Sian didn't see that. She said, "I don't know. We just aren't. He's like my brother."

Melody had always wanted to look at Josh in the way she was hoping Sian would, but she simply didn't. He would have been good for her. She knew that. Everybody knew that, but he was younger than her. Only by about four months, but she'd still started out a grade ahead of him. And compared with her high school boyfriends, Josh seemed so young.

He was her best friend. She could count on him. He knew more about her than anybody else, and she knew the same about him. They shared a connection Melody couldn't afford to lose. Besides, Josh had other girls he was interested in. There was no danger, no attraction between the two of them. There was familiarity and comfort. Melody loved him. Only it was in a very special way. She could see them married as adults. After they'd run away to LA, that is, as they'd always imagined before they got clean. She could even see them with kids, but at almost 16 years old, she didn't know what any of that meant.

For his part, Josh still remembered when Melody had decided she wouldn't speak to him for a week at the beginning of eighth grade. Josh had called her home drunk in the wee hours of the morning one Saturday night. Melody's dad had answered the phone. Josh slurred his words. He slammed the receiver down when Mr. Fisher said his daughter couldn't talk. The man knew his daughter's friend was drunk.

When they showed up at school on Monday, Melody stuck a note on Josh's locker. It read:

I'm in big trouble after what you did this
weekend. Don't talk to me anymore.
- Melody

Josh never even thought about the kind of trouble Melody might have gotten into. Before first period, he stormed into the bathroom, lit a cigarette, and puffed it down in less than a minute. He needed the smoke.

When he left the bathroom, a teacher was walking down the hallway. Looking every which way, she had a determined look on her face. She could smell the smoke wafting through the hall. She stared at Josh as he left the bathroom, but she didn't say anything.

That whole week, every time Josh approached her, Melody turned her back on him and walked away. That was when Josh realized he was in love with her. He could smell the sweet scent of her shampoo as she disappeared. It didn't matter who he was dating. He always had been and always would be in love with Melody Fisher. When she refused to speak to him, Josh's heart hurt somewhere that had never ached before. That was love. Josh was certain of it.

Melody forgave Josh. She didn't want to live without him either. The obvious pain her friend was in hurt Melody's heart too. Only she didn't think it was romantic love that ached for her. It was the loss of her confidante, her best friend. She was spinning freely, whirling out of control without Josh to share her thoughts with.

When she finally approached him again the following Monday, Josh had his head bowed at his locker. He'd gone a week without a single conversation with the one person who brought him life.

"Hey," Melody said.

Josh smiled. His words spilled over one another.

Eventually he told her, "I promise I'll never drink again."

Melody laughed. "Don't make promises you can't keep," she said.

Josh shrugged. "Well I won't call you when I'm drinking again at least," he said.

Melody nodded. She embraced him. They held one another tight. Tears brimmed in Josh's eyes, and Melody closed hers.

Now that they were both clean and sober, Josh remembered that week when Melody had refused to speak with him. He remembered what he'd felt and what he'd learned. When he was alone, he meditated on the reality of it all. He was in love with his best friend. He was certain of it.

In the car on the way back from the beach, Melody sat up front in the passenger seat. Sian was in the back with Josh. That wasn't what Josh had expected, but he took it in stride. He'd thought Melody would sit with him. He'd thought they would laugh and talk together the whole way back to Richmond. Ever since his parents had split up, Josh had spent the past six years hiding his emotions. Nobody could read the disappointment on his face.

They'd already been in the car for a while. Heading north on 95, right around where Denny had pulled the gun on that driver in the silver Nissan, Sian was talking with Josh. He was answering, but even though he was looking at her, he wasn't really thinking about their conversation. He had other things on his mind.

Sian was attractive, but her style was too much like a hippy for the ex-metalhead. She wore an ankle bracelet, Birkenstocks, and a tie-dyed dress. She smelled of patchouli. It reminded Josh of what his mom and her friends had probably been like in college in the 60s in California. As if he had a second set of ears, Josh was trying to make out what Laurie and Melody were talking about up front. But between the air conditioner and the cars outside, he couldn't really hear. Sian required too much of his attention. She was telling him about himself after all.

Sian was saying, "I don't think you need to do much. Becoming what you want the world to be isn't too hard."

"You could even start with a Fourth Step," Laurie said from up front. Her words were much louder than her conversation with Melody had been. Josh and Sian looked up to see Laurie's sunglasses peeking back at them in the rearview mirror. She was smiling. "You do know what that is right?" With authority, she tightened her grip on the steering wheel.

Laurie wasn't a recovering drug addict or alcoholic, but having spent time in Al-Anon family groups after dating Pete's father many years earlier, she knew her way through recovery's 12 steps. She was the one who had originally suggested Pete start going to AA meetings when he left Tucson to move in with her two years earlier. She even took him to his first meetings. That was how she'd met Denny and the rest of the kids. When Denny came up with the idea to start bringing the sober young people down to his beach houses a year and a half earlier—now that both of his own kids had gone off to college, Laurie immediately volunteered to be the girls' chaperone.

Denny never even asked his wife, Grace, if she'd like to go instead. She'd already sacrificed enough during his active alcoholism. She'd stepped over him when he was screaming for a fresh bottle, paralyzed on the floor from alcohol withdrawal while she had to do their kids' laundry so they didn't look like they came from the home they lived in when they showed up at school the next day. She didn't need to keep making sacrifices for him now that he was sober too. Since her own kids were away at college, she didn't have to spend time at the beach with a bunch of children she didn't know. At least that's what Denny told her.

"Yeah, I know what it is," Josh said. He'd heard all 12 steps read aloud at the beginning of every AA meeting he'd been to. The Fourth Step was about taking a "moral inventory" of himself.

"Have you done one with your sponsor yet?" Laurie asked. Melody turned around in the passenger seat. She looked at Josh with a gaze that reminded him of the girl in the passenger seat of Ben's Phoenix the night of his last drink.

Josh looked out the window to his right. The cars were zooming along beside them. He remembered long drives on California freeways with his mom and dad together many years before.

"I don't have a sponsor yet," Josh said. His cheeks reddened. All the other kids had sponsors, somebody they'd picked to guide them through AA's 12 steps. They'd been discussing their experiences with their sponsors all weekend. Pete had admitted his life had changed when Denny heard his Fifth Step a few months before. Matt had mentioned how relieved he'd felt after his first sponsor had led him all the way through the eighth and ninth steps. Even Mikey was struggling with his third step. He was having long talks with Denny about it almost every night. Of them all, Josh was the only one without a sponsor, and he hadn't been willing to admit that to any of them all weekend. Finally saying it aloud in Laurie's car—even though he was embarrassed—a weight lifted off his chest.

"You really need a sponsor," Laurie said. Josh could see the woman's reflection in the windshield. She was wearing sunglasses, but her lips were pursed. "How long have you been coming around now? Seven? Eight months?"

"He hasn't been clean that whole time though," Melody said in Josh's defense.

With Melody coming to his aid, Josh felt Laurie's disdain deflect. The woman glanced over at Josh's friend.

Josh thought it was like being in class and having forgotten his homework—something which had never bothered him when he was using, but now that he was clean always brought the color up in his cheeks. His teachers were never enraged. They merely looked at him with that same sense of disappointment.

Josh was caught. So far he'd skated through sobriety. He'd known there was stuff he was supposed to be doing to ensure he stayed clean, but he hadn't done anything other than stay away from people, places, and things so that he wouldn't pick up a drink. Josh said, "I've only been clean since October."

"Well," Laurie responded, "that's long enough to find a sponsor. Do you want to stay sober?"

Josh thought back to the last few weeks of his using—running from the cops, getting beaten up, having the priest point a shotgun at his face. He remembered his time in Safe Haven and the realizations he'd come to there as well. "Of course I do," he said.

"Then you need somebody to talk through stuff with." Laurie glanced up in the rearview mirror again. Josh was beginning to think what he'd initially mistaken for Laurie's anger might only have been her concern.

Josh said, "I've got friends. I talk with them."

Melody turned around again in the front seat. She smiled at Josh, but he didn't smile back. He was nervous about what Laurie might say next.

Laurie wasn't paying attention to the two teenage friends, though. She was looking at the license plates and bumpers of the cars in front of her. With three teenagers in her car, she didn't want to get into an accident. She said, "But you can't do step work with your friends. If you want to be better, you've got to do better. You need a sponsor. Friends let friends die."

19.

Josh and Sian were sitting on the same couch in Denny's library where Josh had discovered the *Bhagavad-Gita* a few months earlier. He still didn't know what to make of that book. Neither of them were reading. They were facing one another. With her Birkenstocks off and one leg in her lap, Sian had her left arm draped over the couch's back. She was smiling. Josh's hands were in his lap. With pursed lips, he was contemplating his thumbs. He twirled them around one another. They spun like a mini-paddlewheel propelling his hands down the Mississippi River. He might as well call himself Huck Finn. He was reading that book for English class right then.

"So you're happy with your sponsor?" Sian asked.

Josh nodded. He hadn't wanted to get a sponsor. He hadn't wanted to be so vulnerable as to ask somebody to be that for him. To Josh, it felt like asking somebody to be your parent, something that, even sober, he still didn't want. Even after his mom had kicked Bill out, even with as well as Josh and his mom were getting along then, he still didn't want a new parent. Ever since he'd first gotten clean, he'd figured he could do it on his own. But after that drive back from the beach with Laurie and the girls, the thought had nestled into his mind like a splinter—he had to humble himself. For the next two weeks, he picked at that thought during every meeting he went to. But to dislodge it, he needed to take action. There was no way he'd stay sober if he didn't have a sponsor.

Eventually Josh settled on the man who would sponsor him. Men sponsored men. Women sponsored women. So even though Josh would have felt more comfortable opening up to a woman, he still picked a man. The man he chose was Steve S. Everybody in AA went by their first name and last initial. Josh's sponsor was no different.

Steve S. was new to the area. He was about Josh's mom's age, of average height and slim build, with dark hair and dark features. He'd moved to Virginia a few months before. The flattened Os of his midwestern accent reminded Josh of the way his grandfather in Chicago had spoken. Steve wore a Cincinnati Bengals' jacket throughout the winter and spring. Josh remembered the first meeting he saw the man at. Steve was standing outside the Tuesday night meeting introducing himself to everybody who entered the room. He'd shown up early. He was shaking their hands and telling them he was new to the area. He was trying to connect. "I'm from Ohio," he said. In the cold, February air, his breath rose from his lips. As he shook Steve's hand, Josh was impressed. The man's courage was something Josh didn't believe he had.

Steve always went out of his way to say hello to Josh at the meetings they attended together. Josh had no idea why. But the night he decided to ask Steve to be his sponsor, he was grateful the man approached him after the meeting ended. Josh wouldn't have had the courage to do it if things had been the other way around.

"Hey, Josh. How are you tonight?" Steve asked in the

darkness.

There was a large group of people outside. It was early June. The days were getting long and the nights were getting warm. Crickets chirped in the distance. "I'm good," Josh said. He took a drag off his cigarette. Then before Steve simply nodded and walked away as he usually did, Josh blurted out, "Steve, could I ask you a question?"

"Sure. What do you want?"

Josh led Steve over to the same picnic table by the graveyard where he'd had his first conversation with Matt when he was still using. That night seemed so long ago. So much had happened in the eight months since. Steve didn't smoke cigarettes. He'd quit a few years before, but he never admonished Josh for smoking. "It's better than picking up a drink or a drug," he'd once told Josh when the kid had apologized for blowing smoke in the older man's face. "Cigarettes probably kept me sober my first five years. They'll kill you, but they'll kill you slowly. And we need to quit things in the order they'll kill us," Steve joked.

Josh took a seat atop the table. Steve stood with his back to the lights. He crossed his arms. The lights glowed around him like a halo. Bugs buzzed through the glare. Josh bowed his head. "What's going on?" Steve asked.

Josh swallowed hard. "I was wondering if you'd be my sponsor," he said. He didn't look up. "I need somebody to take me through my Fourth Step."

Steve straightened in place. He inhaled deeply. He said, "It would be an honor."

On the couch in Denny's library, Josh said to Sian, "Yeah, I'm happy with my sponsor."

"That's good to hear," Sian said. Brushing her hair back over her shoulder, she tilted her head to the side. She slid closer to Josh. Their knees almost touched. "Have you done your Fourth Step yet?" she asked.

Josh nodded. "Finally." He chuckled. "My Fourth Step's done. Steve and I are getting together to do my Fifth this weekend." AA's Fifth Step was to admit to yourself, your Higher Power, and somebody else precisely what you had done wrong in your life. It was the completion of the Fourth Step, a chance to share what you had realized about your life with someone else. Most often that "someone else" turned out to be the alcoholic's sponsor. Josh intended to continue that tradition.

Josh said, "I call Steve every day. We talk about God and spirituality and all that stuff. All the things Denny," Josh nodded toward the hallway in the distance where their host was hopefully out of earshot, "said he wanted to teach me about." Josh lowered his voice, "But I don't trust Denny. I trust Steve."

Sian nodded. She smiled. Following Josh's lead, she lowered her voice as well. "That's good. I don't trust Denny either, but you need to trust your sponsor," she said. She touched her fingers to the back of Josh's hand. He looked up. Their eyes met. Sian leaned toward him. As her lips nearly brushed against his, Josh leaned back. His eyes were wide. His body was tense. His mouth was set.

Sian laughed. "You don't need to be afraid," she said. She closed her eyes. In a fluid motion, like a cat reaching out for a rat, she moved toward him once again.

Josh leaped up to stand beside the couch. He rubbed his palms down his legs. "I'm sorry," he said. "I don't want to do that."

Sian laughed again. "Is it because you haven't done your Fifth Step yet?" she asked. "Because as long as you've finished your Fourth, that's not a big deal to me."

It was usually recommended to alcoholics to stay out of relationships for their first year in recovery. But if the alcoholic couldn't make it a whole year, it was definitely suggested to make sure to complete your Fourth and Fifth Steps first.

"No. That's not it," Josh said.

With a puzzled look, Sian leaned back onto the couch. "What is it then?" she asked. She slid back to her end of the couch. "You can sit back down," she said. "I won't bite."

After a moment's hesitation, Josh sat back down at the same end of the couch he'd started on. He ran his hands down his cheeks, and he said, "I don't know. It just doesn't feel right."

Sian's expression grew serious. "What? To kiss me or to kiss anyone?" she asked.

Josh sighed. "Anyone," he said.

Sian shook her head. "Have you always been like this?"

Josh thought back over the past few years. He'd dated so many girls, and he'd kissed them all. In fact, up until the past ten months—ever since he'd gone into Safe Haven and he and Carrie had broken up—he'd almost always had a girlfriend. At least, ever since he'd been in seventh grade. And he'd always made out with them—in the hallways at school, in front of the mall, on floors and couches in their bedrooms and dens. That's what made his feelings right then so weird. After everything he'd seen and been through, he longed for some kind of forgotten purity. He chuckled. "No," he said. "I used to kiss everyone."

Sian glanced at him. "I don't know, Josh Marshall. There's something you're not telling me." She narrowed her gaze. "You're an odd one," she said. "That's for sure."

20.

Josh and his sponsor, Steve S., were sitting on patio chairs on the deck coming off the living room of Josh's home. Steve lay reclined, looking up at the stars. Staring down at the blue notebook in front of him, Josh was sitting up straight with a pensive look on his face. Steve had asked Josh to find a peaceful place where they could do his Fifth Step together that Saturday evening. The deck at his own home was the only spot Josh could think of. With the sounds of the tree frogs serenading them from the surrounding woods, it was a pleasant night. The weather was still warm. The lights were on.

The tree frogs started anew. Josh had never tried to write something like a Fourth Step before. He'd never tried writing anything about his life before, and now that he had, he couldn't believe he was going to share it with somebody he hardly knew. He'd heard people around the AA meetings he went to—his friends included—discussing the relief they'd felt after doing their Fifth Steps with their sponsors. Josh hoped for the same. Although, simply by being sober, he'd already felt relief. His life had changed. But still he expected a great revelation at the end of that evening.

The Fourth Step's moral inventory was divided into

three sections: resentments, fears, and sex. The structure was provided by AA's founder Bill W. in the Big Book of *Alcoholics Anonymous*. Josh had spent three weeks writing it into a blue spiral notebook before he fell asleep at night. He'd lie down in his bed, and plumb the depths of his memories to try and reveal who he resented, what he feared, and where he'd been selfish with his behavior.

The first person he wrote down was Kevin McComas from elementary school. He resented Kevin because he'd picked on him and bullied him. That had hurt Josh's self-esteem and sense of security. After writing about Kevin, Josh put down Bill Gladstone, his former stepfather. Bill had invaded Josh's life. He'd changed Josh's responsibilities around the house, and with his attempts at discipline, Bill had even tried to replace Josh's own father. That had damaged Josh's relationship with both his parents, which had also affected Josh's sense of security.

Once he started thinking about his parents, Josh realized he needed to add both of them as well. He resented them for getting divorced. That too had affected Josh's sense of security, which had damaged his self-esteem. Then before Josh knew it, he'd written down nearly everyone he'd ever had an interaction with. It had all damaged his sense of security or his sense of self-esteem. AA's founder had mentioned those two attributes in the group's Big Book, and Josh agreed with him. Those were the two things that seemed to have been at the root of every one of Josh's resentments.

Josh moved onto his fears. The first thing he realized was that he was afraid of almost everything. Some were obvious, like sharks and alligators. Josh had often had nightmares where those animals were attacking him, drowning him, or lying in wait for him. But he was also afraid of his peers. He thought they might make fun of him or that they may never accept him. He was afraid of the future. He had no idea what dangers it might hold. He was terrified of death. It was always waiting there at the end of everything, a maddening nothing of nonexistence. He'd been thinking about and contemplating it ever since his grandfather had died. But most importantly, Josh was afraid of love. It hurt too much.

Finally Josh wrote about his romantic history. He felt shame and guilt over both his desires and his actions. While they were in the thick of their relationship, Josh had never realized that Carrie's actions may have been acceptable to her only because of the abuse her brother had visited upon her. Most of the girls in Josh's classes weren't having sex, but it seemed like every girl Josh was friends with was. And it seemed like every girl Josh was friends with had suffered some sort of abuse. It felt as natural as breathing. Josh's throat closed up. A pit opened in his gut. Josh wanted to cry, but he still refused. He'd cried too much when his dad had left.

On the patio coming off Josh's living room, Steve sighed. "Close your notebook," he said.

Josh looked over at his sponsor. In the nighttime warmth, Steve smiled. He nodded. Josh listened. He closed up the notebook he'd been looking at while the two of them had sat there. Then Josh sighed too.

"That's yours," Steve said, pointing at Josh's blue notebook. "You don't have to share any of it with me… unless you want to. But when we're done here tonight, I don't want you to look at it again. Get rid of it. Throw it away. Drown it. Burn it. Whatever you want to do. After tonight, it's not you anymore."

Josh was surprised. He'd heard stories about marathon Fifth Steps that had gone on for days as sponsors and sponsees had poured through resentments and fears. Now Steve was telling Josh simply to close his notebook and burn it. Josh was confused. He was listening to his sponsor, but he didn't understand.

"Is there anything you want to tell me though?" Steve asked. "Anything you need to get off your chest?"

Josh looked out at the woods surrounding them. Steve's metaphor felt apt. For years, he'd been suffocating. Now that he was sober, he was free. The weight on his chest had already lifted. He dug down deep. Something swam to the surface. The feeling caught in Josh's throat. There was something he wanted to discuss with Steve.

"I've always tried to be so cool," Josh said. "I remember this fight I got into at the mall a couple years ago. This guy kept making fun of me. He kept following me around, saying, 'Hey rock n roller, what's on MTV?' And he'd laugh. Eventually, I turned on him. He was older than me and bigger than me, but we went out into the parking lot, and I hit him with a roll of quarters in each fist. He went down, but he was back up in a second. Luckily mall security came right then because he was about to beat the crap out of me for doing that. But that was all because I was afraid he'd seen something real about me, something I was trying to hide from everybody… Maybe everybody's like that. I don't know."

Steve nodded. Josh exhaled. He said, "As far as my resentments and fears go, they're all the same. I'm not smart enough. I'm not tough enough. It's how I wound up where I'm at today—"

"You wound up where you're at today because you're an alcoholic," Steve said.

Josh paused. He heard his sponsor, but he wasn't sure he agreed. He didn't know what it meant to be an alcoholic. He blinked, and he said, "What I wanted to talk about, though, was something else."

Steve shifted in his chair.

Josh said, "I've only had sex with one person, and she said she wanted to have sex with me. But I can't stop thinking that on some level she didn't really want to have sex with anyone. It was only because she already wasn't a virgin that she was willing to have sex with me, and she didn't really want to not be a virgin. I don't know. Does that make sense to you?"

Steve cocked his head to the side.

Josh looked down. He said, "I thought we were doing something really cool. And now I don't think we were at all anymore." Josh looked back up.

Like a soldier snapping to attention, Steve sat up straight in his chair. He inhaled. He said, "These are complex things you're talking about. I don't think most guys think about them at all. Especially not at your age. I know I didn't."

Josh shrugged. That wasn't the answer he was looking for.

Steve said, "Look, Josh, you're sober now. You've got the possibility of a brand new life ahead of you. The real deal isn't knowing what you want to do about the past. It's how you want to be going forward. That's all there is to it. Some things we do, we have to live with. We can't take them back, and we can't make amends for them. All we can do is try to be different in the future." Steve stopped talking. He bit his lip. He didn't know if he'd said anything helpful. He hoped he had.

Josh leaned back in his chair once again. He wasn't sure about Steve's response. It wasn't what he'd wanted to hear, but it made sense. Josh nodded.

"Is there anything else you feel like you need to tell me?" Steve asked.

Josh turned his gaze inward. He shook his head, *No.*

"All right," Steve said. "In that case, I want you to get on your knees with me." Steve climbed out of his chair. Josh did the same. Steve closed his eyes and bent his head to his folded hands. Josh did the same. "Now take a few seconds to silently say whatever prayer to your Higher Power that you need to say right now."

Josh didn't know what he needed to say to his Higher Power. He didn't know what his Higher Power was. In AA, they said you could use anything—a doorknob, a light switch, God. Anything other than yourself. Before Josh got sober, when he simply showed up at meetings and told them about how he'd been drinking the week before, Josh had always said, *I have a Higher Power who I choose to call Satan.* When he'd done his Second Step with Steve, Josh had told the man he didn't know if he believed in God.

Steve had said, "Think of it like electricity, Josh. Nobody knows what it is, but when we need it, it's there."

Josh hadn't argued. He wanted help. Eventually, Steve had asked Josh to tell him what he wanted his Higher Power to be, whatever that was.

Josh had thought for a moment. "I don't know," he said. "I just don't want to be afraid of anything."

Steve nodded.

"I want something to love me."

Again Steve nodded.

"And I want to know we'll all see one another again."

Again Steve nodded. "Now take all those qualities, and when you pray, pray to those qualities," Steve said. "You can take some away or add more the longer you stay sober."

Josh didn't know many prayers. There was the Serenity Prayer, which many AA meetings started with. There was the Lord's Prayer, which most AA meetings ended with. But to Josh, neither of those prayers seemed right for that occasion. His mind remained empty for a moment. Then he started talking silently—*God, if you're there, please help me be different from how I've been. I've messed up so much, but I want to do better. I want to be better. I don't know what that means, but I believe it's possible. Please help me, God. If you're there, I know you can do it. I believe you can do it. Just take me, God, and make me better.*

With those words, Josh offered himself—in his own words—to his higher power. The next afternoon, before his mom got home from work, Josh burned the blue notebook that had his Fourth Step in it.

21.

The Atlantic rolled underneath him like the wind rocking a baby to sleep in its cradle. Josh's lips tasted of salt and coconut. He wiped away the water dripping out of his nose, slicked back his hair, and repositioned himself astride his surfboard. The sun glistened across the deck. It scintillated on the ocean. Its reflection in the waves blinded Josh without his sunglasses on. Sucking away the fluid to leave only salt, its heat evaporated the moisture off the back of Josh's neck. Josh looked to his left. About ten feet away from him, Matt was perched atop his own surfboard, searching the horizon for their next set. Josh sighed and settled back into his seat. He closed his eyes and swayed along with the ocean like he was back listening to the music at that club he'd gone to with Matt and April in the city of Richmond the weekend before.

They'd seen a local band play live. The music had sounded like the California band the Descendents had met British new wavers The Cure. The vocalist wore his hair in blond dreadlocks. Dealing with the evils of racism and organized religion, his lyrics were socially conscious. He sang about the need for people to define themselves for themselves. He talked about the reasons he wasn't buying into American capitalism. It reminded Josh of the

Transcendentalists he was reading in and out of English class right then, everything from Thoreau's essay *On Civil Disobedience* to Walt Whitman's *Song of Myself.* Josh's body had rocked back and forth to the melodic punk the band had produced. He'd closed his eyes and tapped his palms across his chest in rhythm to their music. He'd bought their independently released four-song EP. And when he got home, he listened to it as carefully as he'd listened to Deicide and Morbid Angel just a year and a half before. But for different reasons. Back then he'd been learning the ways of the left-hand path. Today, he was trying to discover how he could live in a way that—in his eyes— was better.

Josh and his friends were starting to spend a lot of time in the city of Richmond, in a neighborhood called "The Fan," where Virginia Commonwealth University— also known as VCU—was located. That was the college Josh and his friends all believed they'd attend when they finished high school. The neighborhood had an artistic flair. They liked hanging out in a basement college cafe called The Mad Hatter. There, they'd drink cup after cup of espresso and talk about music and movies until the wee hours of the morning. The cafe was located next door to a strip club and underneath a tattoo shop where Josh figured he might someday get his first tattoo. He simply didn't know what he wanted. Nothing was important enough to him yet. Neither Josh nor any of his friends had curfews. After everything they'd been through, their parents were simply happy they were alive and safe. Not to mention, being openly sober, their parents finally trusted them.

A set of waves formed on the horizon. The first two rolled in evenly. As the third wave approached, Josh sat up straighter on his board and leaned forward to spin back to face the shore. He lay down on his chest, brought his hands back over his head, and started kicking. The wave caught him up in its swell. It frothed at the tips. Then it broke. The ocean propelled Josh forward. He stopped struggling. He pushed down on his board and hopped up to stand atop his surfboard and cut across the open water before him.

Josh carved across the wave's face. He couldn't do many tricks, but he could ride a wave. He loved that feeling. Split water trailed along behind him. Ocean spray dotted his chest and chin. He crouched down. His hands hung limp at his sides. The sun scorched his cheeks. He smiled. He didn't have to do anything. The ocean carried him along in its current.

Again, it made Josh think of the spirit of Walt Whitman and his poem, *I Sing the Body Electric*. In the ocean's flow, Josh felt like he could feel the universal procession Whitman talked about. He was a part of it. The ocean was a part of it. Josh's friends were a part of it. Josh thought back to the step work he'd done with Steve. Maybe that was his Higher Power—the perfect motion of the universe itself. There was no way to escape it. It was everything. It was eternal. With a determined look on his face, Josh crouched deeper into the wave.

Without warning, a wall of white water crashed over the nose of Josh's surfboard. The board's pink ombre turned white beneath the wave. A slick sheen lapped at Josh's bare feet. It flipped the board on its edge. The wave closed out. Josh bailed. Still following the direction his surfboard was going in, Josh leaped off the bumpy wax surface coating his board. He dove into the sticky water. The ocean enveloped him in its cool embrace.

Josh resurfaced. He slicked his hair back on his head, blew his nose into his hand, and let the water wash it all away. The ocean glittered beneath the sunlight. Josh grabbed hold of his board's leash and pulled it back over to him. It skimmed across the water. Josh clambered back on. He paddled out to meet up with Matt once again.

The ocean's tug and pull was mild that day. Nothing like that one afternoon the summer before when Melody and April had gone swimming. They'd drifted out into the ocean's depths until they got caught in a riptide. From the shore, Denny was the one who heard them shouting. He pointed at them waving as they were getting dragged farther and farther out to sea. They bobbed up and down, over and under the waves in the distance.

Without hesitating, Matt and Josh each grabbed a surfboard from where it stood upright in the sand. Josh's chest was pounding. A flash of fear split his mind. It really looked like the two girls were drowning out there in the distance. He and Matt dove into the ocean. They paddled out to where the tide had a hold of the two girls. Josh dragged Melody onto his board. April clambered on with Matt. The four of them struggled to cut a 90 degree angle out of the riptide and paddle back to shore.

That night, with water still dripping out of their ears, Melody and April were both convinced Matt and Josh had saved their lives. "I thought we were going to drown for sure," April said. Her eyes were wide.

"Thank you. Both of you, thank you," Melody said. But even though she addressed her words to both of them, she was only looking at Josh.

Josh looked away. He didn't think they'd been as valiant as the girls claimed they'd been. They'd merely acted out of instinct. "Anybody else would have done the same," Josh said. Even though his heart was still throbbing from Melody's gaze.

Laurie, Pete's guardian, looked at him. "But they

didn't," she said. Over Josh's shoulder, she shot a glance at Denny. Josh wondered if the woman was thinking—since it was his condo they were staying at—maybe Denny should have paddled out to help save the girls as well. But Denny had an inner ear issue. He couldn't surf anymore.

Back in the lineup of surfers, Josh closed his eyes and shook his head to either side to drain the water from his ears.

"Nice ride," Matt said.

Josh opened his eyes. His friend had paddled up beside him. Matt was smiling. His frame was small but muscular. Josh never would have known how strong Matt was when he wore a shirt. Josh smiled back. "Felt good," he said.

"Sure it did. You should try doing more than just riding though," Matt said. "Plant your feet and carve it up." Josh nodded. Matt paddled back to about eight feet away from Josh, where he could wait for his own wave.

Since he was older and had been sober and surfing longer than Josh, Matt carried a bit of seniority in their relationship. Josh and Matt were friends, and in that way they were on equal footing. But every relationship has its own dynamics.

From Josh's left, Matt shouted, "Check it out!"

A wave rose out of the water. And even though Josh was tired and his muscles were sore, it looked like a solid ride. Josh felt a surge of energy in his stomach. He wanted to make his friend proud.

Josh spun his surfboard around when his hand slapped flesh. It wasn't his own. Josh looked down. Beside him, a shark's fin rose out of the water. Josh was holding its body. His breath caught in his chest.

He tried not to panic. He'd had run-ins with sharks before, but none of them had ever been that close. He slid down his board. Without paddling too hard, he let the wave catch him in its surge. His surfboard skimmed across the ocean's surface. The spray splashed Josh's nose and eyes. This time, though, he didn't stand up. He was too afraid. Surfers weren't supposed to fear sharks. All kinds of creatures lived beneath the ocean's surface. Like some dude out in California had told Josh the summer before, "A little sand shark will probably only take off your toe, man. It's no big deal."

As he reached the shore break, Josh hopped off his board. Something slippery and alive wiggled out from underneath his foot. With a grunt, Josh leaped through the shallow water. Whatever was under his foot couldn't have been the same shark he'd grabbed earlier. Josh's heart raced. He ran as fast as he could back up the beach, stuck the nose of his board in the sand, sat down in its shadow, and stared across the ocean.

It was alive—the water, the earth, everything. Life hid beneath the mystery of existence. Josh wiped his nose. He felt like Thoreau contemplating experience on the other side of Walden Pond as he stared at the ocean stretching endlessly across the horizon. *Of course, the world is flat,* Josh thought. He closed his eyes. *Any fool looking out to sea could tell you that.*

"Hey, man, what's up?" Matt was walking up the beach from Josh's right. Water dripped off his chest and shorts. It dampened the hot sand.

"Ran into a shark," Josh said.

"Oh," Matt nodded. "Figured it must have been something like that. You got out of that water quick." Matt stuck the nose of his surfboard in the sand beside Josh's board, and he sat down next to his friend. "There's a lot of life out there," he said.

It was as if Matt had tuned into Josh's own thoughts,

but Josh wasn't sure if his friend was only talking about the ocean. He looked away and nodded.

He remembered a moment a couple weeks earlier. He and Melody had been sitting next to one another in History. The bell for class to begin hadn't rung yet. They were talking. "I just don't feel great today," Melody said.

"Physically or your mood?" Josh asked.

"Both," Melody said. "But I guess mainly my mood."

Josh nodded. He closed his eyes. He inhaled deeply. He envisioned a golden light flowing into his nose and filling his body. He exhaled darkness. He inhaled again. The golden energy coursed through his entire being. He centered the energy in his palms. He opened his eyes. He reached out and placed his hands on Melody's arm. He envisioned the energy he'd inhaled swirling through his bloodstream and whirling out his palms into Melody's flesh. There, it flowed through her veins to replenish her own energy.

Melody smiled. "What are you doing?" she asked.

Josh broke his concentration. "It's something I learned from one of Denny's tapes. Energy work. Did you feel it?"

As if she could see Josh's aura expanding, Melody looked around the room. "I don't know," she said. "I guess so." She smiled.

Josh smiled as well. He knew it. With the help of those tapes Denny had given him when the man had first told Josh he'd be his spiritual advisor, Josh was on the verge of a mystical breakthrough. He settled back into his seat as the bell to begin second period rang.

It was like the magic Josh had worked when he'd been a Satanist. Only these spells were bringing positivity into the world. They were driving out the darkness.

"It's crazy all the things we can't see out there," Matt

said.

"What?" Josh asked, startled from his reverie.

"The ocean," Matt said. "There's so much happening underneath us, all around us, every time we paddle out. We don't see hardly any of it."

"Yeah," Josh said. "I was just thinking the same thing."

"I remember one time I was surfing down in Virginia Beach. A stingray swam right underneath me. It was so close I could touch it. It flapped its wings. They rippled through the water." Matt chuckled. He hummed a tune Josh didn't know.

"What's so funny?" Josh asked. He looked over at his friend.

"You never listened to the Grateful Dead much, did you?" Matt asked.

Josh shook his head, *No.*

"What I said just sounded like a line from their song, *Ripple.* I never knew what they were talking about before, but now I feel like maybe I saw it that day in Virginia Beach. Still water ripples because there are things we can't see beneath the surface. All you've got to do is get sober and everything becomes so much clearer."

Josh tilted his head to the side. He didn't know if anything was clearer for him. There was so much to think about.

A couple weeks before, Josh had been hanging out with Melody and her boyfriend, Aaron.

"You see that new Ozzy Osbourne video?" Aaron had asked Josh. They were all squeezing into the cab of his truck. Melody was stuck in the middle. The two guys were on either side.

Josh shook his head. "No," he said. Heavy metal wasn't his thing anymore. He couldn't get Aaron to understand that. Aaron believed the two of them were still into the same stuff, and Josh was never vocal enough about how much he'd changed.

Josh's annoyance didn't register with Aaron though. "I know Ozzy's supposed to be sober now," Aaron said, "but at the end of the video, there's this sound like bong water makes when you inhale. Kind of made me wonder. You know?"

Josh didn't know. He didn't care about Ozzy Osbourne anymore. Ozzy was part of his old life, a negativity Josh didn't want to focus on. He'd left that all behind. There was nothing there to contemplate.

Josh was more interested in discussing Transcendentalist philosophy. He was going through The Bible from cover to cover, trying to understand what people in AA meant when they said the word: "God." He was lost in the books of Hebrew prophets.

Matt stood up. He grabbed his surfboard from where it stuck out of the sand. "Come on," he said. "Let's go find everybody else. I'm hungry."

Josh nodded. He stood up too. He dusted off his hands, and he looked out at the ocean. There was no such thing as still water.

22.

That night, after filling up on pizza, all the kids staying in Denny's condos were out on the beach again. Denny and Laurie, the two chaperones, were back at Denny's place cleaning up after dinner. The sky was dark. The night was warm. Like in a seance, the seven teenagers were sitting in a circle. Melody and Sian were on either side of Josh. Matt and April were next to Sian. Mikey was sitting on the other side of his brother's girlfriend. Completing the circle, Pete was next to Melody. He silently hoped that since Aaron wasn't there, he might be able to convince the girl to make out with him before the end of the night. He didn't stand a chance, though, and he knew it. He looked away from the two friends engrossed in their own conversation. He tried starting a conversation with Mikey about *Dirt,* the newest Alice in Chains CD. Pete wanted to reveal to somebody what he'd realized about that CD. It was a concept album about a drug relapse. But his realization would have to wait. Mikey didn't care. He was talking to his brother about skateboarding, an interest they'd both shared before they got clean.

"I love that song," Melody was saying to Josh.

"I know. It makes me feel how I want to feel when I get married," Josh said. He smiled. He hoped Melody could read between his words. The two of them had talked about getting married before. They'd talked about doing it someday when they were older, when nothing could distract them from each other. What he really meant was: *It's how you make me feel, and I hope I make you feel the same way.* But even he didn't know that was what he meant.

They were talking about the song *Summertime Rolls* off Jane's Addiction's first album, *Nothing's Shocking.* The song was a few years old. The album had come out around the time Josh had first moved to Virginia, but he'd only recently bought the CD. Jane's Addiction had hardly been on his radar when he'd been a metalhead. It was a slower piece with a deep smooth bass line opening it up.

"I know what you mean," Melody said. "When Perry Farrell talks about how—"

"He and his girlfriend aren't wearing any clothes," Josh finished Melody's thought for her. Their eyes met. They smiled at one another. Then they each dissolved into laughter and fell backward separately onto soft beds of sand. It was as if each of them had read something particular in the other's thoughts.

Most of the circle didn't notice. They were all engaged in their own conversations. April, Matt, and Mikey were talking about what they might do next weekend in downtown Richmond. They thought it sounded like fun to ride one of the elevators in a big hotel like The Omni or something. Trying to include himself in their plans, Pete tuned into the trio's conversation. But Sian had been paying attention to Josh and Melody.

I wonder if Aaron can tell how the two of them make each other feel, she thought. She looked down at the sand. She picked a tiny stick out of it. The world grew silent around her. She started drawing lonely patterns. She wished she knew a boy who could do to her what Josh did to Melody, and she wished she could do to a boy what Melody did to Josh.

For his part, Aaron had no idea how Josh and Melody made one another feel, and he didn't care. If he had realized it, he would have been jealous. He would have tried to join them at the beach that weekend, or he would have told Melody she couldn't go. Instead, though, he was back in Potterfield working at his father's convenience store.

Sian looked back up. Josh and Melody were sitting up straight again. They were locked in a serious conversation, but it wasn't private. Sian tuned in to hear what the two friends were saying to one another.

"I think we should do it," Melody said. Her eyes were wild. Her lips were curled. Sian was curious what she might be talking about.

"We'll be just like Walt Whitman," Josh said. Sian couldn't see his face, but she could hear the excitement in his tone. He'd been talking about the poet all weekend.

"And Perry Farrell," Melody said.

"Should we ask anybody else if they want to come, or should we just do it?" Josh asked.

"Let's just do it," Melody said, and she nodded. So did Josh.

The two of them stood up. From the jerkiness of their motions, Sian could tell they were excited. "You ready?" Melody asked.

Josh didn't say anything. He slipped his shirt over his head and off. Melody reached behind her back and undid the strap on her bathing suit. Sian's eyes grew wide. She hadn't expected that. With a simultaneous ring of laughter, Josh and Melody locked eyes, slipped off their pants, and threw them aside. Sian thought she should look away, but her friends were naked in public. If they didn't want to be seen, they could have gone somewhere else. Sian smiled.

Melody reached out and grabbed Josh's hand. The two of them ran down the beach toward the roaring surf.

Pete laughed. "What was that?" he asked.

"Looks like they're going skinny dipping," Matt said. He stared down the beach at his two friends whose bodies were just starting to break the water's surface.

"Looks like I'm going skinny dipping," Mikey said. He laughed. He stood up and started taking his own clothes off.

Josh and Melody were still holding hands when they hit the surf. The ocean slammed into their shins. It cooled their legs. Then it gently lapped at their waists. Neither of them felt so exposed anymore. They let go of each other's hands, and they floated in the waves beneath the moonlight.

"It feels like Jane's Addiction," Melody said. "*Summertime Rolls.*"

Josh smiled. He looked up at the stars. They twinkled in outer space, millions of light years away. He wanted to embrace his friend. He wanted to kiss her in the surf. The desire had never been more overwhelming, not even when they'd lain in bed next to one another sharing cigarettes after a middle school concert. He took a step toward Melody. The whole thing had been her idea. The ocean floor shifted beneath his toes.

A loud splash echoed in the night. Josh glanced back toward the shore. Matt, April, Mikey, and Sian were laughing and running into the water. They were all naked as well. Only Pete sat alone on the beach. His head was bowed. Sand ran through his fingers.

"Figured we'd join you," Matt shouted. He dove into a wave that was breaking against the shore.

"Hope we're not intruding," Sian said, and she smiled.

"You're not," Josh said. He turned back around. Like

a mermaid disappearing into the open sea, Melody was swimming away from him through the crests of waves. She frolicked through the pearls of white water as if she were Aphrodite returning home to Poseidon, relieving humanity of her gift.

23.

"Last night, what was that about?" Matt asked Josh. The two of them were sitting on their surfboards in the ocean.

"It was Melody's idea," Josh said.

Matt smiled and looked away. "Oh, I believe that," he said. "You may have wanted it to happen, but you never would have made it happen."

"What's that supposed to mean?" Josh asked. He scanned the horizon for a non-existent wave.

"It means just what I said," Matt said. He was still smiling.

Josh shrugged.

"What do you think Aaron will think of her idea, though, if he finds out?"

Josh bristled. "Why would he care?" he said. "It's not like anything happened."

Matt cocked his head to the side. As if he were reading something peculiar in the glare of his friend's eyes, he gazed carefully into Josh's face. "I didn't say anything happened. I'm just saying I wouldn't want my girlfriend running naked into the ocean with another guy… even if that guy was her best friend. Do you see what I'm getting at?"

"Well, nothing happened," Josh said again. He turned

his board around and waited for a little bump of a wave to pick him up in its tiny swell. The next wave didn't have enough force for Josh to stand up and ride it to shore. He simply lay still on his stomach on his board, and he let the ocean carry him away from Matt. His friend was asking too many questions, questions Josh didn't want to think about, much less answer.

"I'm just saying you should get out ahead of it is all," Matt shouted at Josh as he rode into shore, but Josh wasn't listening anymore.

Josh had his own relationship with Aaron separate from Melody, and he didn't care much for his friend's boyfriend. Never mind that he'd never cared for any of Melody's boyfriends, but he particularly disliked Aaron. Even though, on paper, the two of them appeared to have a lot in common. They both liked heavy music. Although, since getting sober, Josh had grown more interested in punk and alternative than metal. They were both sober. And they were both in love with Melody. Aaron, however, had no idea about Josh's feelings, and if he did, he never let on. For his part, Josh didn't believe Aaron felt anything like what he felt for Melody. How could he have? Aaron hadn't known her since middle school like Josh had. Aaron hadn't watched Melody struggle with boyfriend after boyfriend while she longed for a more exciting life than what Potterfield County had to offer.

Of course, that didn't mean that Aaron and Josh never hung out. Aaron would pick Josh up sometimes, and they'd cruise around Potterfield together listening to music. Usually, it was something they both could agree on, heavy alternative music like Helmet or Stone Temple Pilots. They wound up at The Mad Hatter in The Fan where they'd drink espresso and keep talking about the music they'd been listening to. Josh even fell asleep on

Aaron's shoulder one night as they drove back from Virginia Beach after a Nuclear Assault show at one of the clubs down there. At first, Aaron shoved Josh's head off of him. It didn't feel right letting another guy snuggle up against him like that. But after the third time, he simply let Josh sleep. It was dark out. Nobody could see into the pickup's cab. Aaron pretended Josh was his little brother.

When Aaron first brought up going to see Nuclear Assault, Josh wasn't sure what he thought of the idea. He'd listened to the band a lot during his metalhead days. He'd even had a patch of their logo on his jean jacket. But unlike Slayer, Morbid Angel, or Deicide, he hadn't given away Nuclear Assault's albums when he got sober. Their music was heavy, but their lyrics were socially conscious. They talked about environmental care and the dangers of bigotry. They asked their listeners to think for themselves and go against the status quo. Josh decided Nuclear Assault still fit with his values. He agreed to go see them with Aaron.

The show was good, but Josh felt uncomfortable. There was a group of kids with bleached hair and big pants—the kind of kids Josh had started growing used to seeing at the shows in Richmond—who kept making fun of the band. Josh felt bad for the guys in Nuclear Assault. He knew they'd come all the way from New York to play that show, and here were these kids who were around Josh's age making fun of them. The music was good. It was just the environment that felt draining. Josh never even realized he fell asleep on Aaron's shoulder during the long ride home.

Once he got back to shore, Josh tried forgetting Matt's advice. He had no intention of sharing the previous night's events with Aaron. Aaron wasn't there. It wasn't his business. Josh picked a tiny stick out from between the grains of sand and started peeling it apart. It split quite easily. If Melody wanted to tell her boyfriend about what they'd all done, that was her prerogative. The stick disintegrated between Josh's fingers.

"Frustration, huh?"

Josh looked up. Sian had appeared beside him. He hadn't heard her bare feet treading across the sand. Casting a shadow over where Josh sat on the beach, she stood with her back to the sun. Josh brought his hand up to shield his eyes. Sunlight broke around Sian's form as if she were the cause of an eclipse. "What's that?" Josh asked.

"The way you're tearing into that stick," Sian said. "It looks like you're frustrated."

Josh dropped the tiny piece of driftwood from his fingers. Where it had originally come from, he'd never know. He wiped his hands off and settled them into the dunes behind him. He leaned back, and his stomach folded to cup a bead of sweat. Sian sat down beside him.

In the distance, in the ocean, Melody and April waded out together through the surf. From where Josh sat, if it hadn't been for Melody's curls, she and April could have been twins. They each waved at Matt as he caught a wave. Josh felt a pang of jealousy with regard to his friend. Then the two girls both leaped in place as a wave crashed before them and white water swirled around their bodies. Josh could tell they were laughing as they picked their arms up and spun around to avoid the cold ocean. "I know how you feel," Sian said.

"I don't know what you mean," Josh said. He didn't speak loudly, and he didn't look at Sian as he spoke. He kept his gaze trained on his friends in the distance.

"We're not like them," Sian said.

Josh looked away from where Melody and April stood

in the surf. "What are you talking about?" he asked.

Sian looked down. "We're thinkers," she said. "We have at least that much in common… if nothing else." She stood up. Without another glance at Josh, she walked off in the direction away from where Melody and April were in the water. She didn't look up, and she didn't look back.

Matt had ridden his wave in. He was talking with his girlfriend and Melody. The three of them were smiling and laughing. Of course Josh was too far away to hear what any of them were saying, but whatever it was, it wouldn't have made sense to him. It never did. He knew that much.

Josh sighed. He grabbed his board from where it stuck up out of the sand beside him. He tucked it under his arm and ran down the beach, back into the Atlantic Ocean, where he threw it before himself and dove through the air to land with a grunt on the deck on his stomach. He started paddling. He floated out beyond the shore break to where the ocean roared in earnest.

HERE'S HOW YOU FLY

24.

The night Josh saw Todd Campbell for the last time was also the last time Melody Fisher ever spent the night at Josh's home. Josh had just returned to Richmond from his dad's place in Southern California. He'd spent the previous month out there. During his last two weeks, Matt had come out to stay with Josh's dad as well. It was the first time one of Josh's friends from Richmond had ever come to visit him in California. Even though Melody had always said she wanted to, ever since Josh had regaled her with stories of Hollywood Boulevard where—in middle school—his dad would take Josh to buy his heavy metal tee shirts.

Josh never thought any of his friends from Virginia would ever spend time with him in the state he still called his home. The two worlds were separate. Virginia was reality, a land of oppression, strife, and discontent. California was a fantasy, a place that only existed in Josh's mind where he could retreat to and remember himself. First it had been the Sunset Strip and Hollywood's promise of heavy metal dreams. Then it turned into an ocean paradise. It had felt strange to be sitting in traffic on the 405 freeway, heading up to Santa Monica with Matt driving his dad's car after a day of surfing at one of the many beaches even deeper in Orange County.

Josh had already been in California for two weeks by the time Matt arrived. The two of them were planning on spending the second half of Josh's summer trip to the west coast surfing and exploring. Matt even brought a handheld recorder for them to immortalize their experiences with. They babbled stories and thoughts into it as they cruised up and down the Pacific Coast Highway, scouring the beaches for the perfect wave, which they never found. Even though they surfed every beach from San Clemente to Huntington. But the first night Matt was there, when he suggested they head down to the pier in San Clemente to see what was going on, Josh wasn't sure anymore what he thought about having invited his friend to join him.

His nights in California were usually spent on the floor of his father's living room watching slapstick comedies and action movies with his dad. It was the only connection Josh still maintained with that giant from his childhood. Just like back home in Richmond, Matt was taking him away from all that and suggesting Josh expand his horizons. Josh was willing to do it, but it hurt. He didn't want to leave his dad alone. As he and Matt pulled out of his dad's driveway, as he watched his father walk back into his home and close his front door, while the Descendents song *Get the Time* blared out of the car's speakers, Josh felt like he might cry. Someday, he told himself, he would get the time to tell his dad exactly how he felt about him.

He and Matt spent two weeks exploring Southern California in ways Josh had never had the opportunity to before. He'd been in fifth grade when he'd left. He hadn't had many friends. He didn't know much beyond the neighborhood he grew up in and where his dad lived now. Matt convinced him to check out beaches he'd never surfed, towns he'd never hung out in, and what little aspects of teenage nightlife they could find when they didn't know anybody else.

By the time they returned to Virginia, they both felt older, wiser, and more experienced. They'd visited another part of the world together. California was a foreign land, and they'd explored it to the best of their abilities.

Laguna Beach held a singular attraction for both of them. It wasn't too far north from where Josh's dad lived. Its restaurants and bars contained a vibrancy the two teenagers wanted to be a part of. The night teemed with wandering partiers of all ages. Surfer kids stole away to the cliffs overlooking the ocean. Girls paraded around the boardwalk. Skateboards crashed and slammed on cement embankments. Josh and Matt made a host of one-night friends, and they had a wealth of adventures that drew them closer than ever before.

Back in Virginia, the summer nights had grown long and hot. You couldn't step outside without breaking a sweat. Josh had ridden into the Fan District in Richmond with Matt. April and Pete had come with them as well, but they were both inside The Mad Hatter right then drinking espressos, talking, and laughing. Aaron and Melody were on their way into the city to meet up with them all as well. Josh and Matt had stepped out to walk down the block and buy a pack of cigarettes. The cigarettes were for Josh, but since he wasn't 18 yet, Matt went with him to make the purchase.

Josh really wanted to quit smoking, but he hadn't been able to. He could feel his life slipping away from him with every inhale. He could feel the smoke choking him every time it touched his lungs. *Soon,* Josh always thought, *I'll be able to quit soon.* But soon wasn't coming fast enough. Josh was terrified of cancer or emphysema. He didn't want to die unable to breathe. He didn't want to die at all. Life held too much promise. But he couldn't resist the desire that was always tingling at the base of his tongue.

As they walked back to The Mad Hatter, Josh noticed a shape he hadn't seen in over a year approaching him. It was an apparition. The kid walking toward them wasn't wearing a leather jacket with tassels dangling off the sleeves. He wasn't even wearing a heavy metal tee shirt. He had on bright green shorts and a pink tee shirt. But his hair was still long, and he was grinning the same grin he always grinned when he was tripping on LSD. Josh recognized his old friend from his heavy metal days, Todd Campbell, coming down the street.

Josh wanted to cross to the other side, but he remembered what Steve S. always said to him—"We work the steps so we can meet people from our past eye to eye. We don't have to duck and hide. We have nothing to be ashamed of." Josh straightened up to his full height. He continued walking side by side with Matt who was reminding him right then about one of their adventures in Laguna Beach.

"Those girls were crazy, man," Matt laughed. Josh remembered the girls Matt was talking about. They'd called themselves Bunny and Fifi. The two girls had jumped into the backseat of their car as Matt and Josh were getting in the front. Bunny and Fifi claimed they were escaping their dates, and they said Matt and Josh looked trustworthy. They told the two of them to drive away before their dates figured out they'd gone missing. "Are your names really Bunny and Fifi?" Matt asked.

The girls assured them both they were. They even produced IDs confirming their assertions. "But those could have been fake," Josh's dad said when they told him the story the next morning at breakfast. Matt and Josh had laughed with those two California girls all through the night. "I really can't believe they trusted us enough on sight just to hop in our car."

"Yeah," Josh said. He smiled. But he was watching Todd as he approached. He wondered if his old friend would still recognize him. Josh's hair was different. His clothes were different. He even carried himself differently. He used to walk with the same coyote hunch Todd walked with. Now Josh stood straight.

Matt noticed Josh's stiffness. As if he had just confronted Vlad the Impaler, his friend walked like his head was on a pike. Matt was getting ready to ask him, *What's up, man?* Then the longhaired guy in the pink shirt and green shorts who was approaching them suddenly addressed Josh. "Hey, buddy," he said.

Matt wasn't sure if that was a friendly address or not. He bristled for the fight he thought might be approaching. He didn't know how the two teenagers knew one another, where they had crossed paths in the past. Matt was prepared to defend his friend. But Josh merely smiled an awkward grin. "Hey, Todd," he said back to the longhaired kid. A thousand thoughts passed through his mind. Tina had cheated on Todd with Josh when the older headbanger had been locked up. Josh didn't know if the address had been friendly or not.

But as if only a day had passed since they'd last seen one another, Todd's smile grew even larger. He asked, "So what have you been up to?"

Matt relaxed.

Josh shrugged. His life was so different from the last night he'd seen Todd, the night when he'd eventually wound up in Safe Haven. He had no idea where to begin. Tears built behind his eyes. He had no idea why. He simply said, "Nothing much, man. You?"

Todd shrugged as well. But Josh knew some of what

his old friend had been up to. Shortly after Josh had stopped hanging out with them, Todd had gotten Tina pregnant. She'd dropped out of school to raise the baby, and Todd had disappeared from her life. "Oh, you know," Todd said, "little bit of this, little bit of that." He chuckled nervously. The laughter rattled in his throat. It was a disconcerting sound.

Josh smiled. "It's good to see you, man," he said.

"Likewise," Todd responded. Without another word, he continued on his trek down the street.

Josh turned to watch his old friend wander away. What an anticlimactic way to end their relationship, Josh thought. He wondered what Todd had had to live through since Josh had last seen him. He remembered the lie he'd told his mom when they'd been caught sleeping out in the woods the week before Josh went to Safe Haven.

As Josh watched Todd disappear down the block and around the corner, Aaron's truck pulled into a parking spot across from them. Melody got out on the passenger side. Josh went to shout, *Hi!* But she looked like she might be crying. Josh was confused.

Aaron ripped the driver's side door open and slammed it closed behind himself. The crash of the door reverberated down the street. Melody jumped in place, and Aaron came careening around the front of the car. He wasn't drunk from alcohol, but he was drunk from rage.

Matt was just starting to ask, "Who was that?" When Josh quieted him with a wave of his hand.

Aaron flew around the front of the truck. He was saying something to Melody, but Josh couldn't hear what at that distance. Then Aaron was standing over Melody. He grabbed her by the shoulders. Josh was frozen. Aaron drew Melody toward himself. He released her by shoving her back into a brick wall.

Pete, who had just stepped out of The Mad Hatter to smoke his own cigarette, shouted at Aaron, "What are you doing, man?" The tall lanky kid took a step toward Melody's boyfriend. Aaron gauged the size differential between himself and Pete and decided against a confrontation. He quickly retreated back to his truck, started it up, and drove away.

As Aaron pulled away, Josh broke his trance. He shook his head and ran over to Melody who was slouched over, crumpled at the base of the brick wall. He couldn't believe what he had just witnessed.

25.

"This reminds me of old times," Melody said to Josh. Through her smeared mascara, she smiled.

They were lying on their backs in his bed together, staring up at a crack in the ceiling. Melody was supposed to be sleeping in the guest room, but they'd always drifted off together in his bed. Eventually one of them would be startled awake. Melody would shuffle off to the guest room down the hall. Josh's mom would never know.

Josh's eyes filled with tears. There were so many things he wanted to say to his friend. He wanted to tell her he was sorry about what had happened earlier that night. If he'd been closer, maybe he could have gotten to her before Aaron shoved her into that wall. He wanted to tell her how he'd always felt about her. Aaron never needed to be in the picture. He wanted to thank her for everything she'd done for him over the years. He wouldn't be who he was without her. He wouldn't be clean without her. There were so many things Josh wanted to say, but he was scared. Once he made his truth manifest, the fantasy could be erased. Sometimes, truth requires fantasy. "Yeah," Josh said. The words caught in his throat. "It sure does."

There was a heaviness to their evening together.

Neither of them knew it was the last time Melody would ever spend the night at Josh's home. They were both preoccupied with their own reminiscences about everything that had happened earlier that night. Aaron had driven away. Pete had rushed over to pick Melody up from where she'd fallen. Josh and Matt reached her shortly after that. Melody threw her arms around her friend. "I want to get out of here," she'd sobbed to Josh.

Matt ran back into The Mad Hatter to tell April what had happened. He was going to drive the two friends back to Josh's home on the other side of the river. Melody didn't even stop off at her mom's to grab a change of clothes. At first she wasn't sure if she would spend the night. But as the evening wore on, she eventually called her mom to say she'd be staying with Josh. She didn't have to tell her mom anything specific about what had happened. Her mom respected her daughter's decisions. The woman wondered if Aaron would be okay with it, but she knew and trusted Josh.

"Do you remember the night after that AC/DC concert?" Melody asked.

Josh smiled. "We were so stoned," he said.

"We were," Melody agreed. "And your stepdad was such a creep."

Josh remembered how Bill had stared at Melody when she'd come home with them. The man even adjusted his rearview mirror to see the middle school girl's legs better in the backseat. He and Melody had talked about that when they'd returned home. She'd shivered with disgust as she recounted how it had made her feel. Rage had roiled Josh's gut.

Melody rolled over to her side to face Josh. He rolled over toward her as well. She smiled. They were so close to one another. All Josh needed to do was lean his head forward, and their lips could easily meet. "That was before I met Aaron," Melody said. Josh frowned. He flopped back onto his back.

"What are you going to do?" Josh asked.

Melody shrugged. "I don't know," she said. She pursed her lips. She tilted her head to the side, but she didn't say anything more.

"You need to break up with him," Josh said.

Melody nodded, but she still didn't say anything.

"After this, after tonight," Josh said, "you need to break up with him."

Melody nodded again. "We've been through so much together," she said. She was nearly whispering.

At first, Josh didn't know whether his friend was reminiscing about him and her or talking about herself and Aaron. But with the distant gaze she directed at the ceiling and the fact that she wasn't looking at him, Josh realized she was referring to the latter. He scrunched up his lips. He rolled away from Melody onto his other side.

He was trying to help her. It wasn't only for selfish reasons he wanted her to break up with Aaron. Aaron didn't understand Melody. He didn't care about her. The latest incident was another example of what Josh already knew. Aaron didn't care about anybody other than himself. The guy's conversations proved that. He was always telling Josh how hot other girls were. He had a crush on Sian. Josh was certain of that. When Josh had mentioned to Aaron in an offhand way how Sian had come onto him, Melody's boyfriend had said, "I'd get with her in a second. And I've got a girlfriend."

When the two of them went to that Nuclear Assault show together, Aaron's biggest critique of it had been that there weren't any pretty girls there. "Nothing nice to look at," Aaron said. He smiled. That made Josh angry. On the ride home, he closed his eyes and drifted off to sleep rather than listen to any more of what the guy had to say. He was dating Josh's best friend. In his bed with Melody, Josh hoped he was different from Aaron.

Josh had never told Melody what he really thought of Aaron. He'd never revealed to her the conversations Aaron had had with him. Given his own feelings about Melody, he didn't think it was appropriate. She'd trust him. He had to be sure his motives were pure. Matt knew the truth. Melody didn't. Besides, if anything ever did happen between the two of them and he'd been bad-mouthing her current boyfriend, it would cast Josh in a negative light. Better to swallow his words and maintain silence than to risk letting his own feelings influence his counsel.

"That's no excuse for what he did tonight," Josh said. Anger burned in his chest. He couldn't allow Melody to forgive Aaron. He couldn't let that happen.

"You're right," Melody said. "I know you're right," Her voice trailed off into nothing. She stared at the ceiling.

The tension in Josh's chest released. For a moment, he believed he was getting through to her. But that belief only lasted for a moment.

"It's just," Melody said, "you really don't understand this one."

"What's there to understand?" Josh said. "You won't tell me what you two were arguing about." Josh glanced over at Melody. He had an idea what they might have been arguing about though. Sian had probably tipped Aaron off to how Josh and Melody had started the skinny dipping party at the beach. He assumed Melody didn't want to tell him because she didn't want him to feel responsible. "And that's okay. Because it doesn't matter. Nothing's an excuse for what he did to you tonight."

"You're right. I know you're right. But still… you won't understand."

"Try me."

Melody turned over on her side. She gazed deep into Josh's eyes. She was looking for something there. Emotions welled inside of Josh. They were so close to one another. Their foreheads were almost touching. He smiled. Melody found what she was looking for in Josh's gaze. "You won't understand," she said, and she rolled back over onto her back to stare once again at the ceiling from behind the mascara smeared around her eyes.

IV.

26.

The teacher was drawing two lines in the shape of a cross on the clear plastic sheet broadcast to the front of the classroom by the light from the overhead projector. Josh had never put much thought into how those devices worked before, but today he was enthralled. It was as if he were stoned. Even though the previous fall he'd celebrated the third anniversary of when he wound up in Safe Haven. He hadn't touched a drink or a drug since that night.

The overhead projector was an interesting piece of machinery. A light shone up from the bottom to illuminate a clear plastic sheet placed on a glass tray. The light made visible anything that was drawn on the sheet to a mirror above. The mirror reflected the image onto a screen at the front of the classroom. In this instance, the image projected onto the screen was the cross.

Josh was intrigued. He was still slowly making his way through The Bible at night, but he'd recently reached the gospels. As his math teacher drew that shape on the overhead projector, Josh couldn't get the idea of the crucifixion out of his head. That cross meant something. He settled deeper into his seat and began paying attention.

"So this horizontal line," his math teacher said, "is the x-axis."

Josh opened one of his notebooks, something he rarely did in school. He wasn't usually interested in taking notes. This lesson was different though. Josh drew the teacher's cross on a piece of paper. He labeled the horizontal line: X.

"And this vertical line," the teacher continued, "is what we call the y-axis."

Josh labeled the vertical line: Y.

A hand went up in the corner.

"Yes," the teacher said. He set his erasable pen down on the projector.

"Why do we call them x and y?" Scott Smith asked.

"That's a good question," the teacher said. "I don't have an answer though. We just do."

The class snickered. Scott turned red. Josh stared at the design on his paper. He was thinking. He started chewing on his pencil. The imagery of the cross had Josh thinking about spirituality. There was a mystery there to understand, but Josh didn't know what it was.

The teacher drew arrows on either end of both lines. "We put these arrows on here to show that each line goes on forever." Then he made hash marks across both axes. "And we can number each of these marks in order," he said. "One, two, three…"

Josh followed his teacher's instructions. Something was coming into focus, some truth he had never seen before.

"This point is zero," the teacher said, pointing to where the two lines intersected. Josh marked the spot on his own diagram as well. "So if I count over two spaces on the x-axis and up five on the y, I wind up right here." The teacher put a dot on what seemed a random point in the blank space between both axes. He said, "We label this point like this: 2,5. Does that make sense?" The class nodded.

Josh was following his math teacher's instructions when it all became clear to him. The x-axis was the physical dimension. The y-axis was the spiritual dimension bisecting our physical experiences. Where the two axes intersected—the zero point—was an individual, a sacred heart, the peaceful center of our existence. Josh leaned back in his chair. Then as if he could see the mysteries manifesting themselves in the physical world, he leaned closer to his desk.

His teacher was explaining how there were four distinct quadrants created by the two axes, but Josh saw something else. He saw four dimensions of existence surrounding the individual created by the intersection of the physical and spiritual planes. The positive numbers were positive experiences—both spiritual and physical. The negative numbers were negative.

Each point in all the corresponding planes were other beings on their own unique journeys. Everybody's zero point was in relation to their axes as well. The more spiritually positive the being, the more angelic it might be. The more negative, the more demonic. The more physically positive the being, the greater impact it had on the physical plane. The more negative, the less.

Each of these beings could draw a person toward them—either unconsciously or of the person's own volition. Just like the line Josh's math teacher was drawing right then from the zero point to the point he'd already marked on their coordinates: 2,5. A person's consciousness traveled across those lines to intersect with other creatures. And for those moments, while that connection existed, the person existed in a different place.

They were more positive, more negative, more physical, or more spiritual.

Josh saw all of existence rotating around him at fixed points on the Cartesian coordinates. There were angels and demons. People with more or less power over him. Spiritual presences that could impact him to greater and lesser degrees. People who could ascend to heavenly heights. And individuals who descended to demonic depths. There were Todd Campbell and Carrie Condrey. There were the kids from Safe Haven—David and Diana, the kids from AA—April, Sian, Pete, Aaron, Matt, and Mikey. There was Bill Gladstone and Josh's own mother and father. There was Melody Fisher…

Melody never spent the night at Josh's house again after that night two summers earlier. Josh only saw her once more that entire summer, and he hadn't seen her since. They'd said good morning to one another the following day. Melody had been pensive as Josh's mom had served them breakfast. She'd asked if Josh's mom could bring her home shortly after that. Josh called her that evening. Her mom said she was out with Aaron, and Josh was livid.

He didn't speak with her again until she called him the next night. She wanted to stop by his place to talk. Josh said, "Sure."

Aaron dropped Melody off that night, and Josh was enraged. He'd never been able to save Carrie, and he wouldn't be able to save Melody either. As if the two girls ever needed him to save them.

Melody got out of the truck. Aaron pulled away as Melody walked up to Josh's front door. "What is that about?" Josh asked as he opened the door.

Melody stepped inside. She plopped down on Josh's grandfather's chair in the foyer. "I told you, you wouldn't understand," she said.

Josh shook his head. He stepped away from her and leaned back against the wall.

"I'm pregnant," Melody said.

A pit opened in Josh's stomach. He slid down to the floor just as Melody had done when Aaron had thrown her into that wall outside The Mad Hatter. "Are you sure?" he asked.

"I'm sure," Melody said. With a heavy exhale, she looked down at the ground. She didn't look back up for a while.

Josh didn't say anything either. He stared at the emptiness overtop his friend, where a halo might rest if Melody were in truth the angelic being Josh had always imagined her to be. Her revelation didn't change that belief. It merely complicated things.

"What are you going to do?" Josh asked.

Melody let out a long sigh. "I'm keeping it," she said. Melody had had abortions before. One in middle school. Two more during her brief stint with Aaron already.

Josh nodded. "That makes sense," he said.

"I'm dropping out of school," she told him. "I won't be there next year."

Josh nodded again. He couldn't imagine life in school without Melody, but he didn't have a choice. He knew her mind was already made up.

"It's no big deal," she said. "I'm two years behind where I should be now anyway. I mean, failing last year again… I'll be a year behind you even." Melody laughed, but it was a pitiful attempt to keep her spirits up.

"I guess that's why you have to stay with Aaron then, huh?"

Melody nodded. "I don't really want to," she said. "Especially not after the other night. But we have to give it a shot. For the baby's sake."

"For the baby's sake," Josh whispered. He looked up at the ceiling. He said, "If you stay with him, I can't be your friend anymore."

Melody nodded. She understood.

That conversation was the last time Josh had seen or spoken to Melody Fisher. She was gone from his life as quickly as she'd entered four years earlier, and Josh missed her terribly. He knew she'd had the kid. Matt had bumped into Aaron at a meeting. He'd told him. Aaron was simultaneously angry and proud to be a father, Matt had told Josh. As far as Josh knew, Aaron and Melody were still together.

27.

As Josh walked the halls of his high school after class, he couldn't get the thought of those Cartesian coordinates out of his head. The day was over. He had math for sixth period. Josh was on his way to his first rehearsal for the first play he'd ever landed the lead role in. He was going to be Romeo in his high school's production of *Romeo and Juliet*.

Josh had started taking drama as an elective the year before. He'd signed up because Melody had signed up as well at the end of sophomore year. It had been her idea for them to experience art in that way. Josh had thought it would be fun to do it with his friend. It might bring them even closer. But Melody had dropped out of school before their junior year began. Josh took the class alone. But he still managed to grow enthralled with the theater.

The school's theater teacher, Ms. Bachman, was a well-loved icon. Kids listened to her with rapt attention. She was an artist, a visionary, a director who pushed her pupils to explore what they were capable of becoming. The students who stuck with her department listened to her and looked up to her as only fledgling artists could with one who had experienced and inspired so much more.

At the end of junior year, Josh had tried out for a role in his high school's production of *Grease*. It had taken all the courage he could muster to walk into that auditorium and give the performance he was asked to give in the audition. He'd wanted to run away when he'd stepped on stage, but he didn't. He'd hoped to wind up Danny Zuko, the leader of the play's T-Birds gang, his hero when he was in fourth grade, but he'd wound up a lesser T-Bird with only a handful of lines. It was humbling. Josh didn't have the singing chops to land a larger role.

The experience, however, was still magical. Josh fell in love with theater in the same way he'd fallen in love with music and surfing. He'd given the bit part his all, and it had been worth it. He sat in the wings getting into his character. He did exercises to remain focused. Inscribed on the walls of the theater were the words: *On this stage, a frightened young mind was lost.* Josh agreed. He'd discovered a new type of inspiration, one he'd never experienced before.

Out of nothing, the cast and crew birthed an entire world. Everything was make believe. Nothing was real—not the props, not the characters, not even the emotions. But the fabrication was still experienced. Josh imagined it must have been how his favorite bands felt when they wrote a song. It was probably how Walt Whitman felt when he completed a poem. It felt like something akin to LSD. It might have even made sense out of God—a kernel of truth wrapped in nothingness.

Josh intended to study theater in college the following year in New York City where he'd gotten into his first choice school early decision. He'd just recently found out, and he couldn't believe it. At the end of that summer, in August, Josh would be packing his bags, and his mom would be driving him—just like she'd done when they'd gone up for his artistic review—all the way to the city where he'd move into a dorm somewhere in downtown Manhattan, a place he'd never imagined himself living until—at his mom's behest—he'd researched the best theater programs in the United States.

The application process had been unnerving. Josh wasn't sure if he had the talent he needed. He'd only ever auditioned for one play before in his entire life. And he hadn't even landed the lead role in that. But Annie Stein—Josh's mom had gone back to her maiden name after divorcing Bill—had been adamant about Josh following his desire. He'd worked day and night with Ms. Bachman to prepare his monologues for artistic review. He'd never wanted to become anything other than a rock star before, but now he wanted to be an actor. He was excited. He was afraid.

However, right then he was still in the second semester of his senior year of high school and enthralled with the spiritual implications of Cartesian coordinates. *What did it all mean?* He opened the side door to the auditorium. His math teacher had continued after explaining the x- and y-axes. He'd told them about the third dimension, the z-axis. Josh had seen that as the mind bisecting the body and spirit in its own right. Josh shook his head. The rest of the play's cast was already on stage. He didn't know the girl playing Juliet.

Her name was Jenn Bryant. She was a senior as well, but Josh had never had a class with her. His high school had more than 2,000 students. He'd seen her around the halls. But he'd never really met her.

Jenn was short, barely over five feet. She had dirty blond hair and the alternative style of a mid-90s hippie. She wore corduroy, patchouli, and Birkenstocks. Josh had changed since the days when he'd first met Sian at the beach in North Carolina. He found Jenn attractive. She seemed introspective and serious. He was looking forward to working with her. He was looking forward to getting to know her.

Josh still hadn't had a girlfriend since Carrie at the beginning of ninth grade, before he'd gone into Safe Haven. He hadn't even been out on a date with anybody. Matt always got on his case about that. But Josh was adamant he wasn't interested. He'd been too enamored with Melody, too damaged by his previous relationship, and too confused about how he believed people should conduct themselves. Between Carrie's private suffering, his mom's marital devastation, and Melody's experiences, Josh had no idea what he believed about the value of romance anymore. How ironic that he'd been able to channel the necessary energy to land the role of Romeo. The desire must have still remained latent in him somewhere.

"Well hello there, Romeo," Ms. Bachman said as Josh entered the theater. Her voice was bright. Josh smiled. His thoughts of Cartesian coordinates vanished. He was on stage. He had lines to memorize, an entire persona to become.

Jenn Bryant stood beside Ms. Bachman. Looking straight at Josh and twirling a stray strand of her hair, she appeared pensive. "You know Juliet, your costar," Ms. Bachman said. Nobody went by their given names in Ms. Bachman's theater, only the names of their characters.

"I don't think we've ever met," Jenn/Juliet said.

"We haven't," Josh said. "I'm Josh. I mean Romeo." From a distance, he waved.

"Wonderful!" Ms. Bachman said. "Tybalt, Benvolio, and the rest of the Capulets and Montagues are already working on their opening scene."

A group of actors stood at the far end of the stage. "*Do you bite your thumb at us, sir?*" one of them asked.

"You can meet your families later. For now, you two," Ms. Bachman nodded at Jenn and Josh, "need to meet one another... officially. Come with me."

Ms. Bachman led Jenn and Josh out of the theater. The two teenagers followed her across the hall to the drama classroom. There she handed them each their own copy of the script for *Romeo and Juliet* by William Shakespeare. Josh held the pages with reverence. Ms. Bachman had taught him words were holy things, and he'd learned how to perceive that. Ms. Bachman sat down backwards in a plastic chair, rested her arms on the chair's back, and told Jenn and Josh to open to a specific page. "Now take her by the hand, and read," she said.

Josh glanced from Ms. Bachman to Jenn and back again. After having worked through his artistic review monologues with her, Josh knew when Ms. Bachman wasn't about to be dissuaded. He grabbed Jenn by the hand, cleared his throat, looked down at the script between his fingers, and said his lines.

The language didn't make sense to his ear, but he understood it on a deeper level. It was as if he weren't speaking English—although he was. Of course he was. But right then he was speaking a language that resonated with him somewhere deeper than the words themselves. This was sound. It was meaning. Josh felt the words in a way he'd only ever experienced music before.

Jenn responded to him. Her words were liquid gold. Josh realized she could feel them as much as he could. It wasn't just his own voice. He and Jenn were speaking on a wavelength he'd never communicated on with another, not even Melody. They went back and forth looking at each other and living inside the other's words.

When the script suddenly said: *He kisses her,* Josh paused. He didn't know what to do. His lips hadn't touched another's since Carrie's. He didn't know how to do something like that anymore. He didn't know if he wanted to do something like that anymore. A sternness hardened his chest. This wasn't what he'd imagined his next kiss would be. Something meaningless, delivered by a character other than himself in a classroom overlooked by a teacher. He needed it to be true. He glanced over at Ms. Bachman.

"Just touch your lips to her cheek," she whispered. Josh took a deep breath, and he did it.

The warmth of Jenn's cheek was invigorating. Josh pulled away. The caress of her skin still tingled on his lips. He looked down for his next line.

Ms. Bachman clapped her hands once. "Perfect," she said. The spell was broken. Josh stepped back. He smiled. He turned red. Jenn Bryant looked at him perplexed.

28.

Josh was riding with Matt in the same dingy, white Ford Escort his friend had always shown up at AA meetings in. Deep bass thumped out the speakers. It rattled the doors and the trunk. The two friends were listening to *Illmatic* by New York rapper Nas. Matt had grown into a huge hip hop head. He was always sharing his discoveries with Josh. Sometimes it struck Josh how much he'd changed in the years he'd been clean. As a middle school metalhead, he never would have listened to rap. He'd loved The Beastie Boys and Run-D.M.C. in elementary school. They'd been his favorite artists before he'd discovered Guns N Roses, but in Potterfield County, metalheads didn't listen to rap music. Todd Campbell had even helped Josh finally destroy his copy of Run-D.M.C.'s *Raising Hell.* Josh shook his head at the memory.

As he listened to Nas's rhymes, Josh thought of the lines from Shakespeare he'd read in rehearsal earlier that afternoon. He remembered Jenn's responses, and he smiled. Then his gaze grew serious. He believed rap was poetry. He'd argued with his mom about it. But it was only in that moment he realized poetry was rap. Shakespeare was meant to be spoken. It was meant to be heard. It wasn't created to be taught in a classroom like when Josh had read *Antony and Cleopatra* in English the year before. The words weren't dead on a page. They were living emotion crafted to affect a person's feelings. Like Nas, Shakespeare was saying something. If only Josh had the ears with which to hear.

"What's up, man?" Matt asked. "You seem even more lost in your head than usual."

"Nothing much," Josh said. He frowned. He shrugged. He looked out the window. On Potterfield County's backroads, trees blurred past the windows. No other cars passed them. It was as if they were the only people who existed. Josh thought back to Jenn. Her interpretations of Shakespeare's rhythms had captivated him. He understood them as clearly as if she'd been singing the song *Waterfalls* by TLC.

Josh shook his head. He didn't want to share his real thoughts with Matt. He was afraid he couldn't articulate them right. And even if he could, he was afraid his friend wouldn't understand. He blurted out, "I had this crazy dream last night."

"Yeah?" Matt said, giving Josh an invitation to continue his train of thought.

"Yeah," Josh said. He settled deeper into the passenger seat, and he continued, "I dreamt that I was in my house. Where my mom and I live now. Not our old place where we lived with Bill, but the new place. And the yard was all nice and clean. Until I turned the corner.

"Around the corner was a whole part of the yard I'd never seen before. But everybody else—all our neighbors and stuff—could see it. It was overgrown and a mess. I stepped into that part of the yard, and I realized there was a whole other part to our house there that we'd never really moved into either. It was sterile and sophisticated. Like my great-grandmother's place in Chicago.

"As I followed that new part of the house around the corner, I saw there were steps leading down into a basement that we don't have. I followed the steps down. I was afraid, but there was light. So I figured it was all right. But I was still afraid to be going down there like that. I kept saying, *I'm an angel of light. Nothing can hurt me.*

"The basement was multilevel. It was so spacious. My fear disappeared. *We could have parties down here,* I thought.

"But when I got down to the bottom level, I realized there were Nazis hiding in our house. It was weird. Because the whole dream was in color, but the Nazis were in black and white. We didn't invite them in. Somebody named Chris had put them there. I simply knew that was true. The way you know things in your dreams are true even though nobody ever explained them to you."

Matt nodded.

Josh went on, "I was scared of the Nazis. Because I knew they wanted to hurt me. But a flaming sword appeared in my hand, and I waved it at them. I kept saying over and over again, *I'm an angel of light.* The Nazis still wanted to hurt me, but they couldn't because I was fending them off with my flaming sword.

"I backed away from the Nazis. I went deeper into the basement when everything got dark. I mean it was pitch black down there. Even in my dream, I couldn't see anything. I got really scared. *The devil lives down here*, I thought. *He put the Nazis here.* Then I realized, *The devil is named Chris.* But I kept repeating, *I'm an angel of light.* I waved my flaming sword everywhere. It couldn't light the dark, but if I kept swinging it, I believed even the devil couldn't hurt me.

"That's when my flaming sword went out. I was

terrified of the Nazis, of the devil, of everything. Then I realized I was the devil.

"I turned around. I felt wings come out my back. I was huge and powerful. I started walking back out of the basement. But now I was repeating over and over again, *I'm an angel of darkness. I'm an angel of light.*

"I got back to where there was light in the basement. The Nazis were gone. My flaming sword was gone. I looked in a mirror. But the face looking back at me wasn't mine. It was familiar, but it wasn't mine. *Is that me?* I thought. *No, it's Chris,* I said out loud. The guy, the devil, whoever he was, who put the Nazis in my basement.

"I moved out of the way of the mirror so that Chris couldn't see me. I was afraid of him. But when I moved, Chris moved. That's when I realized I was Chris. I started laughing.

"I walked out of the basement and back up to the main level of my mom's and my house, laughing the whole time about how scared I'd been of myself.

"Then I realized there were all these attic levels to the house that I'd never noticed either. I started walking up a set of stairs that we don't have to explore them. But before I got into the attic to see what was up there, I woke up."

Matt was smiling. His hands were gripping the wheel. Nas was booming. "That's a crazy dream, man," Matt said above the bass. "What do you think it means?"

"No idea," Josh said. "There was this one guy who hit me the last night I was using. His name was Chris, I think," He bit his lip. He was afraid he'd wound up revealing more about himself than he'd intended. "But that couldn't mean anything," he said with a whisper that was barely audible above the music.

"So what's up with Juliet?" Matt asked, reading his friend's mood and quickly changing the subject.

Josh's stomach dropped. "What do you mean?" he asked.

"You said you were excited to work with her. How's that going?"

Josh relaxed. "Good," he said.

"Anything going to come of it?" Matt asked.

Josh straightened in his seat. "I don't know, man. You know how these things go."

Matt smiled, but his eyes remained serious. "Yeah I know how they go." He flexed his fingers around the steering wheel.

Matt and April had broken up. She'd decided it was time to move on. She'd left Matt, and she'd left AA. Neither Josh nor Matt had heard anything from her since her last meeting. She'd vanished. There were rumors she'd started shooting heroin. But none of the kids in AA wanted to believe that.

"Well just give it some time," Matt said. He'd been out on a few dates since April. Usually with girls from his college classes. But he hadn't really connected with anyone.

Josh leaned deeper into the passenger seat. He wanted to laugh off what Matt was talking about and tell him, *Hey man, it's not like I'm really into her or anything.* But he was afraid his friend would quickly see through that charade and continue his line of questioning. Josh could only deflect for so long. Matt would eventually discern the truth. Instead Josh chose the safe route and simply nodded. "I like this album a lot," he said. Now he was the one trying to change the subject.

"Yeah. It's cool right?" Matt said. "As raw as Wu, but as skilled as Tribe."

Josh knew the artists Matt was referring to—Wu-Tang Clan and A Tribe Called Quest. Like Nas, both of them were from New York. The city Josh would be calling home in a little over six months. He'd spent hours dissecting their beats and rhymes from the same seat in Matt's car he was riding in right then. He was excited. He agreed. Still unable to comprehend how far he'd grown from who he'd been, he smiled. There was no dissembling there. That grin was only for him.

29.

Josh and Jenn were alone in the drama classroom together. The rest of the cast was across the hall on stage with Ms. Bachman in their high school's theater. They were working on the party scene. So far away from them, Romeo and Juliet were rehearsing their famous balcony scene.

Josh spoke a few lines to start the scene. Juliet was standing behind a faux-Chinese screen Ms. Bachman kept in her classroom for purposes like this. As Juliet stepped out from behind the screen, in their collective imagination, she appeared on the balcony before Romeo. Josh's breath caught in his throat. His eyes grew wide. He wasn't sure anymore whether he was acting or truly feeling. He stumbled over his lines. But their rhythm felt as natural as if they were flowing freely from his own mind.

Juliet hadn't noticed him yet. She was staring off into space. She spoke. Josh heard her voice. It interrupted his monologue. It interrupted his thoughts. He stage-whispered to himself again. Lost in her own reverie, Juliet stared beyond him as if he weren't there. Josh was enamored by her lips, her jaw. The look in her eyes was sincere and powerful. He wondered what she was thinking. He poured his heart into his words.

Then she spoke again. Josh listened. She pined for him. Emotions welled inside of him. It was different from what he'd felt for Carrie. It was different from what he'd felt for Melody. It was more pure than the former, more subtle than the latter. The two actors' monologues went back and forth until Romeo finally revealed himself.

Juliet noticed. She squinted and verbally accosted the boy she imagined to be standing in the shadows beyond her balcony. Romeo spoke again. He stepped out from behind the chair the two of them were imagining was a tree. In reality, it hadn't hidden him at all. But as far as the two actors were concerned, Romeo might as well have been invisible. Jenn's eyes grew wide as she recognized her love. She panicked at what awaited him in the halls behind the balcony she believed herself standing upon. She spoke. She told him her fears, and Romeo assuaged them.

As Romeo and Juliet went back and forth speaking to one another, they inadvertently approached one another. The balcony wasn't there in reality, and the two actors weren't experienced enough to hold their positions solely in their imaginations. It was as if a tractor beam were dragging them closer together.

Before the two imagined lovers knew what was happening, they were speaking their lines directly into the other's face. They were grinning at one another. Josh swallowed slowly. A sensation tingled in his stomach. He didn't know if Juliet felt the same, but she looked like she did. Josh spoke his lines.

Then Juliet whispered, "You never kissed me on the lips."

The spell was broken. Josh blinked. He said, "That's not in the script."

"I know," Jenn said. "But it's true. You only kissed me on the cheek."

Josh swallowed slowly. He looked down. He looked back up. Jenn was staring into his eyes. He could see something glinting between her iris and her pupil. That must have been her soul. A memory of sitting on a couch and watching *Star Trek* while Carrie Condrey's mom got up to go to the bathroom flashed through Josh's mind. He leaned forward. He pressed his lips to Jenn's. It was the first time he'd done something like that since before he'd been put in Safe Haven. At first he remembered the sensation of Carrie. Panic welled inside of him, but then he forgot. He closed his eyes.

Fireworks exploded in Josh's stomach. They lit his mind. As his costar stood up on her tiptoes to respond to their kiss, a smile tickled Josh's lips. It felt like an eternity that the two of them possessed one another. Then Josh remembered where they were. Ms. Bachman could enter at any time. He didn't know what she would say to greeting them in that manner.

Josh opened his eyes. He pulled away from Jenn. But he was still smiling. He was holding her hands in his. They were so warm. Her pulse throbbed below her thumb. Jenn was smiling back at him. She reached up. She wrapped her arms around him, and she hugged him close. Beneath their clothes, he could feel her heart beating against his chest.

30.

Josh and Matt were sitting at the base of the free paint wall on Lombardy St. in the city of Richmond. It was one place where the city didn't care if there was graffiti. Kids could paint there all night without any fear of being arrested. Of course that wasn't the only place where Matt painted. But it did allow for a more leisurely atmosphere.

Josh took a sip off his soda. The wall above them was a huge, unfinished mural of a black man astride a horse. The piece was meant to look like it was one of the statues on Richmond's Monument Avenue. Only, instead of being a Confederate general riding the horse into battle, it was a man who looked like a triumphant Tupac Shakur with his fist raised in power. As if for inspiration, Tupac's newest album, *Me Against the World*, was playing out of a boombox running on batteries beside the two friends.

"You know, there was this old LA metal band, Lizzy Borden," Josh said, "they had a song called *Me Against the World* too. I haven't heard it in a long time, but I bet it holds up. It was a solid track."

Matt nodded. He took a sip off his own soda. "It doesn't mean the same thing though," he said.

Josh frowned. He looked down. "No," he said. "It doesn't."

Matt wasn't the artist doing the large piece. He was working on a smaller piece down on the bottom right-hand corner of the wall. It was just his tag, "Lost," done in brilliant oranges and yellows. The "L" in the tag turned into the "s." The top of the "s" became the crosshatch for the "t."

Matt had been planning the piece for weeks, drawing it in his notebooks, putting it up in no time on trains pulling into the city before they ran back out onto the open rails. Beneath the moonlight, the graffiti had shone like paintings on rusty canvases at the Virginia Museum of Fine Art. It brought the city to life. Like some forgotten hobo, it traveled along the rails and told stories across the country. At any number of railroad crossings, drivers waiting for a passing train might see one of Matt's pieces clatter by. They might notice it. It might speak to them. It might inspire them. It might not.

Josh however was inspired, and not only by Matt's graffiti. It was life itself that held him in its thrall and lent an air of invincibility to his actions. He took another sip off his soda. Maybe the drink's caffeine was affecting his brain. He craved a cigarette, but he knew he could make it longer before he needed one. He inhaled deeply. The naked air tasted of life rather than death-breeding smoke. Josh smiled.

Matt glanced at him over his shoulder. "What's so funny?" he asked.

"Nothing," Josh said. "Everything." He laughed. "I just feel good, man. Better than I have in years. Better than I felt after finishing my Fourth Step. I don't know why."

Matt smiled at his friend's mood as well. "Maybe it's because you finally kissed Juliet."

"Maybe," Josh said. He sighed. "But why should that make such a difference?"

"I don't know," Matt said. "It just does. It always does."

"I guess you're right," Josh said.

"Of course I'm right." Matt turned to face Josh. "You're smart, man. But sometimes you just can't see. People need people. We need friends. We need girlfriends and boyfriends. We can't survive completely on our own. You should know that by now."

Josh nodded. He remembered his thoughts about Cartesian coordinates from a few weeks before. But then he forgot. Matt was still talking.

"It's the connections that make life worth living. That's what people like us don't have when we're using drugs and alcohol. Real human connections."

Josh looked down at the asphalt they were sitting on. He didn't say anything, but he couldn't help thinking Matt was wrong. Josh frowned.

"You don't believe me?" Matt asked.

Josh shrugged. "I don't know, man. Me and Melody, we had a real connection when we were using. And now—"

"But you never told her how you felt. How real of a connection could that have been?"

"I don't know if I felt that way when we were using. It wasn't until after we got clean that I—"

"Look inside yourself and tell me if you really believe that," Matt said.

Josh frowned again. Maybe his friend was right. Maybe he'd always felt that way about Melody, and he never told her. Josh sighed. That lent an air of insincerity to their entire relationship. It was like Matt said. He and Melody couldn't have had a real connection based on that kind of falsehood. Josh stood up.

"Where are you going?" Matt asked.

"Just to walk around a bit. I need to think about what you said."

Josh walked Richmond's empty streets. The city was abandoned, desolate, and boarded up, the murder capital of the United States. Josh should have felt more fear walking the city's streets alone at night. But he didn't. It was where he lived. It was where he was coming of age. It wasn't where he would have chosen to. If it had been up to him, Josh never would have left Southern California. But it was where it was happening.

He kicked a can across the sidewalk. It skidded along the concrete and out into the street. No cars drove by to run over it and crush it. Richmond's roads didn't get much traffic. Josh sighed. In less than six months, Richmond wouldn't even be where he resided anymore. That was hard to believe. He'd gone through so much there, even more than he'd ever gone through in the state of California that he still considered home.

A man on the corner asked Josh if he could spare any change.

"Not tonight," Josh said.

The man stepped out of the shadows of a tree overhanging the sidewalk. "You know I carry a gun right?" he said. "If I wanted what you got I could take it, but I won't. I'm polite. I just ask. So why don't you give me some money."

Josh swallowed slowly. "I really don't have any money," he said, which was the truth.

The man stepped back into the shadows. He straightened his shoulders and rose to his full height. Josh tried his best not to cower down into himself. He knew that wasn't how to defuse the situation. Then the man said, "Okay, I believe you." He walked away from Josh down the sidewalk.

For the first time during his stroll after leaving the graffiti wall, Josh felt afraid. But he kept walking.

He'd experienced so much in the years he'd spent in Richmond and the counties surrounding it. He'd started drinking, started doing drugs, made out with girls, been beaten up, gone to rehab, discovered sobriety, spirituality, and so much more. But now it was all coming to an end. A dingy Ford Escort on the roads of Potterfield County wouldn't be where Josh would ramble his daily thoughts out to his best friend anymore. The clubs on Grace Street in The Fan wouldn't be where Josh would discover new music anymore. His friends were all going to VCU. Josh was moving to New York City. He swallowed slowly. His throat felt dry. Jenn Bryant wouldn't be coming with him. He'd spent seven years in the suburbs of Richmond waiting to meet her. And now she wasn't coming with him.

What Matt had said resonated with Josh. It was true he needed connections in his life. And it was true he'd never been entirely honest with Melody about his feelings. Josh's ears burned with shame. He knit his brows, thrust his hands deeper into his pockets, and kept walking. He wouldn't make that same mistake again. Not with Jenn. Not with anybody.

Eventually Josh would have to turn around. Matt had driven him down there. Matt needed to take him home. But not yet. Something was on the edge of Josh's consciousness, something he couldn't quite put his finger on. But it was important. It meant something. Josh needed to understand.

He was on the same block as The Mad Hatter, the cafe they'd all been hanging out at the night Aaron had thrown

Melody into that wall. Josh's gut tightened. He crossed the street. He touched his fingers to the same brick wall Melody had crumpled at the base of. He'd just bumped into Todd Campbell that night when everything happened. That meant something, but Josh didn't know what it was. He slid down the wall to sit on the sidewalk. He was sitting in the same place Melody had sat when Josh's spell had broken, when he'd run across the street to pick her up from where she'd fallen. Josh brought his hands up to his face. He dropped his head forward. He inhaled deeply. When he exhaled, despite his earlier exhilaration, he started to cry.

It was as if a lifetime of pain had broken through the dam inside of him. Josh's shoulders heaved as he stared at the concrete beneath him. He sniffled as snot dripped from his nose. He wiped his eyes. He couldn't remember the last time he'd cried.

31.

It was Saturday. Romeo and Juliet were heading in from Potterfield County to Maymont Park in the city of Richmond. With Japanese gardens, Italian gardens, an old manor home, and even a small zoo, the park was an entire world unto itself. Josh and Jenn had both been there before, but never together. Josh had often gone there with Melody, Matt, and April during his first year of sobriety. He'd only been back a handful of times since. The journey was bitter sweet.

Josh had his driver's license. After waiting a whole year past when he was eligible for it, he finally got it the year before. But next year he wouldn't even need it. Not in New York City. He wondered if he'd remember how to drive when he came back home for winter break, if he came back home for winter break. He tightened his fingers around the steering wheel as he pulled into one of the parking spaces in Maymont's lot.

He and Jenn were in the middle of a serious conversation. "I would just tell them it was a lie," she said as Josh pulled his keys out of the ignition.

He turned to face her from the driver's seat before

opening his door. "But why?" he asked. "I don't see what the big deal is." He got out of the car.

Jenn got out on her side as well. As she closed the passenger door, she said, "Because once your kids know you've lied to them, why would they ever trust you again?"

Josh pressed the lock button on his side of the car. He closed his door as well and put his keys in his pocket. "But is telling them about Santa Claus really lying to them?" he asked.

"How could it not be?" Jenn asked. "And even worse, it's a lie that all of society has been conspiring to make them believe. It's horrible."

Josh smiled. "Really? Horrible?" he asked as they headed across the parking lot and into the park.

"Yes, horrible," Jenn said. They were walking along a gravel path. A bright green lawn stretched out to either side of them. Trees dotted the horizon in all directions. The manor house towered over them. The main zoo was ahead of them. To their right, at the top of the hill was the petting zoo. They turned left. As they walked down the hill, they passed the deer enclosure. They stopped to look. "I'm serious about this," Jenn said.

Josh stepped back from the chain link fence separating them from the deer. The animals were so majestic. Forget about the carnivores. With their racks of horns, these were the true gods of the woods. He looked at Jenn. She was frowning. Josh sighed. "I know," he said. "I just never really thought about it before. Telling my kids about Santa Claus, that just doesn't seem like that big of a deal to me."

"But it is. Do you remember when you found out Santa Claus wasn't real?"

A distant look passed over Josh's face. He remembered cuddling up with his mom one night when he was much younger. She told him there was no man who delivered presents on Christmas Eve. There was only the spirit that she gave her gifts to him with. Josh had already suspected it, but that night, he cried himself to sleep as a little bit of magic left his world.

"It hurt, didn't it?"

Josh shrugged.

"I mean it was the biggest lie anybody had ever told you up until then right?"

Josh nodded.

"And I'm sure you couldn't figure out why nobody had ever just told you the truth. That's the beginning of the end of our relationships with our parents, with everybody. We learn we can't trust our whole society after that," Jenn said. "And I don't want to treat my children like that. I want them to know they can believe in me at the very least."

"I never thought much about it," Josh said. "But when you put it like that, it really doesn't make sense why we'd want to start our children's lives off with a lie."

Where they stood across from the deer, Jenn nestled against Josh's ribs. "I knew you'd understand," she said. Josh looked down at her again. She was smiling. He smiled back at her.

"I want to see the bears," Jenn said.

They started down the path again. They passed some cages with a couple vultures in them, some foxes, even a hawk. "I'm glad you stopped eating meat," Jenn said.

"Me too," Josh said.

"There's just not enough room to live in there," Jenn said, nodding at the hawk in the cage. "She can't fly. Imagine if she was a chicken. She'd live her life in something even smaller than that until somebody killed her for no reason that she understood. And what's even worse, her babies would be raised the same way."

Josh stared at the bird. She was looking back at him. She would eat him if she could, if she was big enough and hungry enough. Josh knew that. He respected that. But he didn't want animals and their children to be raised for the sole purpose of being eaten by him anymore. He didn't want to eat something that had never been free. He didn't want to eat something he hadn't had the courage to kill himself. Josh hadn't eaten meat in over two months by then. He was hungry, but he didn't want to do it. He didn't want to enslave what he believed were his co-evolved beings. Someday the hunger would subside.

It had started when he'd been petting his mother's cat—a former stray she'd inherited from a friend. The cat had lived its youth in a dumpster in an alleyway. Josh felt a great deal of empathy for it.

That afternoon the cat had been sitting in a warm patch of sunlight on the back deck. As Josh stroked the cat's fur, he felt its leg. The bones beneath its muscles felt no different from a chicken's. Josh wondered what made a cat so special that he wouldn't eat it. Why were birds, fish, cows, and pigs disposable. Josh recoiled at the thought. He hadn't had a bite of meat since that moment.

He'd been inspired by Jenn. She was vegetarian too.

They reached the enclosure with the bears. "They have more space in there," Jenn said. "But it's still not all that much."

Josh nodded. He agreed. The bears appeared free. But they could only roam so far.

"I just wish we didn't have to keep animals in cages," Jenn said. "I wish we could just let them be."

One of the bears stood up on its hindlegs to grab a branch from a tree above. For a moment, Josh saw that two-legged animal with a face like a dog as the inspiration for a werewolf. That thought made him relate to the bear in some sort of way. Josh shook his head.

He and Jenn picked up their pace and rounded a corner on the path to enter the Japanese garden. Josh inhaled deeply. The world smelled of cherry blossoms. "I've always loved this place," he said.

Jenn looked over at him. She could tell from his expression he was experiencing something profound. "Any particular reason why?" she asked.

Josh shrugged.

Jenn inhaled deeply. She looked up at Josh. She smiled. She grabbed him by the hand and pulled him deeper into the garden. "Let's go," she said.

Josh followed. They traipsed along a stone path, overtop a bridge under which giant golden koi were swimming. The bridge zigged and zagged. Josh stopped to look at the fishes' movements below the surface of the water. He remembered a conversation he'd had with Matt years before on the beach in North Carolina. Something about the Grateful Dead and ripples in the water or something like that. Jenn tugged at his arm. Josh forgot his train of thought and moved along.

Up a hill, the pair made their way into the Italian garden. It was rich with foreign flowers. A long pergola, with roses growing overtop it, extended before them. Josh and Jenn stepped beneath its vines. They walked from one end to the other.

"This is where we'll get married," Josh said only half in jest. He was smiling.

"I don't want to ever get married," Jenn said.

Josh looked down at her. His girlfriend was so filled with opinions and life. He believed he might even love her for that. That one word, love, had been so hard for him to fathom since before Carrie Condrey had left him. Josh frowned.

Jenn continued, "Besides you're moving to New York in the fall. By this time next year, you probably won't even remember who I am."

"I'll remember you," Josh said.

Jenn looked up at him and smiled. Her gaze melted any stony regions remaining in his heart. "It doesn't matter," she said. "We'll both have so many new adventures between now and then, we'll hardly even be the same people. Let's simply enjoy our time together now."

Jenn grabbed Josh's hand. They stepped out from underneath the pergola and back into the sunlight.

Josh gazed across the field before them toward a gazebo in the distance. He felt what Jenn was saying. Her words melted his heart so completely that nothing was left. He knew it was all true. They'd go their separate ways soon and maybe never see one another again. The two teenage lovers were as star-crossed as their characters— Romeo and Juliet. But neither of them sought the same permanence as the play.

Once again Josh remembered his realizations concerning Cartesian coordinates from a couple months before. The thought had returned to him often. Now, however, he grasped its significance. He straightened up where he stood. His axes were shifting once more. As they'd done many times before. The people who inhabited his proximity would soon be different. He was about to be introduced to a number of new points on his graph.

32.

The cast started by walking through Potterfield Town Center in their costumes. They came from different entrances, but they coalesced in the food court, where one of the cast members said to another, "Do you bite your thumb at us, sir?"

A staged fight then ensued in the middle of the diners and shoppers going about their Saturdays. As the prince appeared to stem the violence, the mall's patrons quickly picked up on what was happening. They settled into a spellbound audience as the abridged play spun out around them into the famous balcony scene.

The cast hid Juliet behind them before she stepped out to appear before Romeo. As a mere human, Josh was speechless when Juliet revealed herself. As an actor however he said his lines.

For her part, when Juliet repeated her famous line about why Romeo had to be named Romeo, she felt heavy with emotions. They dripped through every word she spoke. Like Romeo himself, she knew that in real life their love was as doomed as the characters they portrayed. But still the show must go on.

The audience was enraptured. Potterfield Town Center was impressed with Louthain High School's performance. But one person in particular made her way to the front of the crowd. She stood directly in front of the players. Not because she wanted to be seen, but because she couldn't believe who she was seeing.

Josh recognized Carrie Condrey immediately. Unlike Josh, she looked no different than she had three and a half years earlier. She even wore the same clothes—black jeans, black hi-tops, black tee shirt. She had the same haircut: long with bangs. It was as if time had not passed for her as it had for Josh. His words stuck in his throat, but he'd been trained. He completed his scene as he'd rehearsed it.

When the teaser was over, as the narrator announced to the audience that the entire performance of *Romeo and Juliet* could be seen at Louthain High School the following weekend, Josh left his troupe. He made his way through the crowd until he stood behind her. "Carrie?" he asked.

She turned around.

Josh's stomach went into a somersault when he realized it was really her. They'd been through so much together in such a short time so long ago. And so much more had happened in the years since they'd last spoken. Josh had no idea what to say, but he didn't have to say anything. Carrie spoke for him, "It's nice to see you, Josh," she said. "Your play was good."

Josh shook his head. This wasn't the conversation he wanted to have with her at all. "I didn't know if it was really you," he said.

"It's really me," Carrie said, "in the flesh." She looked down at the ground. She turned the toes of her shoes toward one another.

"There's so much I want to say to you," Josh said.

"You don't have to," Carrie told him.

"You—"

"It doesn't matter. That was all a long time ago. We had fun. That's all that matters."

"Did we have fun?" Josh asked.

Carrie didn't say anything. "How's Melody?" she asked.

"I haven't seen her in a couple years," Josh said.

"I'm sorry to hear that. You two were always so close," Carrie said. "I thought you'd wind up married."

Approaching them, Josh made out the shape of Carrie's mother in the distance. She was pushing a baby in a stroller. Josh felt a panic in his chest as if he still weren't allowed to see his old girlfriend.

Carrie pointed over her shoulder. "I need to go catch up with my kid," she said. "Grandma can't take care of him forever."

Josh was dumbstruck. "Your—" he didn't say anything else. The gravity of his life before he got clean hit him in a whole new way, differently than when he'd bumped into Todd, differently even from when he'd found out Melody was pregnant.

"See you around, Josh Marshall," Carrie said. She wandered away. As she did, she added, "By the way, you look great. Whatever you're doing, keep it up."

Josh didn't even have the chance to say thank you. He mumbled the words, "Good bye," to her back.

"Who was that?" somebody asked from behind Josh. Carrie's spell over him broke. Josh looked in the direction of the new voice. It was Jenn. She was smiling at him.

Josh smiled back. "Nobody," he said. "Just an old friend."

33.

Josh was nervous to be at the cast party for *Romeo and Juliet*. It was being held at Barry's, the lighting technician's, house. Leaving their home to the teenagers, his parents had gone out for the evening. Since high school had started, Josh had never been to a party that wasn't being thrown by his friends in AA. It was nerve-racking for him to be around his peers who were drinking alcohol and smoking marijuana. He hadn't smelled that subtle scent in over three and a half years. It filtered in through the door where Tybalt and Mercutio were out on the back porch. Josh wanted a cigarette to combat his memories of that substance's sensations, but he'd quit those as well around the time he went vegetarian. It had been more than three months. At 90 days clean, he'd gotten a red poker chip as a sobriety marker at an AA meeting. Nobody gave him anything for 90 days off nicotine. He rubbed his fingers together and licked his lips.

"Are you having fun?" Jenn asked him.

"Not really," Josh said.

"Let's go outside then," Jenn said.

"Could we leave through the front door?" Josh asked. "I don't really want to walk by them smoking pot."

Jenn nodded.

They sat down on an old metal swing set in the backyard. It must have been Barry's when he was a child. Like Josh, Barry didn't have any siblings. The swing set hadn't been used in years, but his parents had kept it around because they couldn't believe their child might never swing in it again, even though Barry was heading off to college at James Madison University in the fall.

Josh twirled circles on his swing. Jenn pushed herself lightly back and forth on hers. Even though she'd just turned eighteen, her feet barely touched the ground.

"I wasn't having much fun in there either," Jenn said. "Parties aren't really my thing."

Josh snorted a short laugh. "Well they're definitely not my thing," he said. He mumbled, "I have no idea what I'm going to do in college."

"You'll figure it out," Jenn said.

"Drinking and drugs are just such a part of it all."

"If I can do it, you can do it," Jenn said.

Josh nodded, but he wasn't sure if she understood. Jenn didn't drink or smoke because she didn't want to. Josh wanted to. He really wanted to. It was just that he couldn't. He had to admit that to himself. It was the only way he might be able to keep himself from using drugs and alcohol again. Josh pursed his lips and exhaled. He'd come too far. He'd experienced too much. As far as he could tell, drinking and drugs had upset his whole life. He was so different from who he'd been when he'd been using them. He felt like he did when he was a child again, when his parents had been together and his grandfather had been alive. He remembered what Carrie had said when he'd bumped into her while they were performing at the mall—*Whatever you're doing, keep it up*. Josh hung his head.

Jenn said, "We need to talk though."

Josh looked up. "I know," he said. But he didn't want to talk. At least he didn't want to talk about what he was afraid Jenn wanted to talk about.

"The show's over," she said.

Josh nodded.

"And that means the school year's coming to an end."

Josh nodded again. A distant memory from many years earlier surfaced in his mind. His dad came into his bedroom in California. *—I have to leave tonight*, the man said. Josh didn't respond. He just nodded.

Jenn inhaled. "And that means we should probably stop hanging out so much."

Josh remembered his dad saying *—I need you to know this isn't your fault*. Josh nodded.

Jenn sniffled. "I've had so much fun with you, Josh," she said. "But if we keep hanging out, it's going to hurt too much when you go to New York."

—Your mom and I simply can't seem to work things out right now. "I don't have to go to New York," Josh said.

Jenn smiled. "Don't say that. You do have to. I need you to become a famous actor so I can say I knew you when."

Jenn grabbed his hand. Josh's fingers melted in her warmth. He hung his head. He tipped it to the side. He closed his eyes. Tears built behind his eyelids. He sniffled to keep them down. Jenn leaped off her swing. She embraced him. She started crying. "I think I love you, Josh Marshall," she said. "And I can't bear to fall more in love with you before you do what you need to do."

Josh returned Jenn's embrace. But he couldn't tell her

he loved her. Not right then. He'd never told her that before, and this couldn't be the first time. Not when they were breaking up. They held onto one another for what felt like it was close to eternity. But of course, it wasn't. Then they let each other go. Jenn wiped her tears. "I'm going to go back inside," she said. "Will you be okay?" she asked him.

—*Will you be okay*, his dad asked him.

Josh nodded.

He sat outside on that swing set for a while after Jenn left. He knew he needed to get out of there. The smell of marijuana in the distance was calling to him. The laughter of buzzed teenagers reached him. He needed to call somebody. He didn't really talk to Steve, his sponsor, much anymore. But Matt would listen. Josh's car was parked down on the street. Matt probably wasn't home. But Josh knew where he'd be, down at the free paint wall on Lombardy St., working on a new piece of graffiti.

Before he left, though, as he pushed himself back and forth on that swing for a little while longer, in his mind's eye, Josh saw a set of Cartesian coordinates receding away from him. A different set grew closer. In fact, there was a whole world of Cartesian coordinates approaching him. For a second, he didn't know if the coordinates were moving toward him or if he was moving toward them. Then with the swing soaring beneath him, for the first time in years, Josh felt like he was flying.

34.

Josh had expected her to look different. He'd thought a lifetime had passed since they'd last seen one another. He'd finished high school. He'd gone off to college. Now here he was, returned for his first winter break. They should have been middle aged. She shouldn't have looked the same. But there she was, sitting next to him on the couch in his mom's family room looking exactly like she had the last time he'd seen her. Her hair might have been cut a little shorter now, but underneath the long coat she'd taken off when she'd entered, she wore bellbottoms and a midriff tee shirt. This was definitely Melody Fisher.

Josh smiled. Melody smiled back at him. She rubbed her arms. "Are you cold," Josh asked her. He moved to stand and turn the thermostat up.

"No." Melody shook her head. She said, "I'm good. It's just nice to see you." She smiled again. She hadn't taken her eyes off Josh since she'd first entered his mom's home a few minutes earlier.

When she greeted him at the door, it was like she'd never seen him before. Then as if she'd been there a million times, she went straight to the same couch they'd always sat on at Josh's old place, the house he and his mom had shared with Bill Gladstone. Melody had never been to Josh's mom's new home. Even though Josh and his mom had spent his last two years of high school there. Josh and Melody hadn't seen one another that whole time.

Josh settled back into place on the couch beside Melody. "It's nice to see you too," he said. "I couldn't believe it when you called." He looked down. "For the longest time, I never thought I'd hear your voice again." A vague memory from middle school popped into Josh's mind, but he quickly set it aside. He didn't need to remember anymore when he first knew he was in love with Melody Fisher.

"I always knew you would," Melody said. "Because I knew I needed to hear yours."

Josh smiled sadly. It was Melody's turn to look down. "So you made it through your first semester of college?" she asked.

Josh nodded.

"Sober?"

Josh nodded again. But sadness washed over his features. It had been a difficult few months. He loved his classes. But he didn't have many friends. Life in the dorms revolved around drugs and alcohol. Two things that Josh refused to partake in. He went to meetings, and there were young people there. But he hadn't connected with anybody like he had with his friends in Potterfield County. He shook his head and changed the subject. "You broke up with Aaron?" he asked.

Melody nodded. "It didn't work out," she said, "just like we all knew it wouldn't. Even a baby couldn't change that."

Josh nodded. "What were you two arguing about that night at The Mad Hatter anyway? You never did tell me."

Melody sighed. "You didn't figure that one out yet?"

she asked. "He wanted me to have another abortion."

Josh swallowed slowly. "I think I get it now," he said.

Melody nodded. "But I couldn't do that," she said. "I couldn't do it again."

They sat quietly together once again for a little while. Then Josh asked, "How is the baby?"

Melody smiled in a way Josh had only ever seen her hint at before. Her gaze became more luminous than Josh had ever seen through all their years of friendship. "He's good," she said. "And his name is Noah."

"Right," Josh said. He looked up at the walls surrounding them. "Where is he?"

"Noah's with my mom, his grandma. I'd like you to meet him. He's wonderful."

Josh nodded. But he couldn't believe he was talking with Melody Fisher about her child. For Josh, parenthood, like adulthood itself, was a distant place. Adults were still, on some level, the enemy. They weren't to be trusted. And in order for one to be a parent, they had to be an adult first, regardless of their age. Time meant nothing when it came to raising a child. The experience was everything. Or so Josh imagined.

"I'd love to meet him," Josh said.

Melody smiled again. "Noah," she said. "You'd love to meet Noah."

"I'd love to meet Noah," Josh repeated. He smiled back at her, but unlike with Melody, Josh's smile died at his eyes.

Melody noticed. "I think you'd really like him," she said. She looked down.

Josh inhaled. He glanced up at the ceiling. After a short chuckle, he said, "Hey, did I tell you I got a tattoo?"

Melody shook her head, *No*. "Where is it?"

Josh pulled up the sleeve of his tee shirt. On his

shoulder were the x- and y-axis of a set of Cartesian coordinates. On them was the plotted point: 2,5.

"Cool," Melody said, "what's it mean?"

"It's hard to explain." Josh pulled his sleeve back down. "It's just something I've been thinking about for a long time." He turned around in his seat to better face Melody. "I got it in the Fan at that place above The Mad Hatter."

"Where we used to always hang out," Melody said.

"Yeah," Josh said, but his voice trailed away. "Where we used to always hang out." A wash of memories intruded upon his thoughts. But one in particular stuck in his mind's eye. He shook his head to clear it from his internal vision. "Did you ever hear about what was really going on with Denny and Laurie?" he asked.

"No," Melody shook her head. "What?"

"They were having an affair," Josh said.

Melody looked at him. Her eyes grew wide. "How'd you find out about that?"

"Matt told me. Apparently Mikey walked in on them one time while we were all down there. He didn't tell anybody for years. Eventually he told Matt."

"Wow, I had no idea."

Josh nodded. "Nobody did. That whole 'taking sober kids to the beach thing,' that was just a cover up so they could get time together away from Denny's wife. Can you believe it?"

"I can believe it," Melody said. "But can you believe it?"

"Not really," Josh said. "It really bothers me."

"Why is that?" Melody asked.

Josh said, "Think about it… under the pretense of a good deed, they were doing something horrible."

"Did Denny's wife ever find out?"

"I don't know," Josh said. "But that doesn't change the fact that they did it. I haven't spoken to Denny in years."

"Wasn't he your spiritual advisor or something like that?"

"Something like that," Josh said.

Melody shrugged. "Well, it also doesn't change the fact that they did a lot of us a lot of good."

Josh looked over at her.

She said, "Would you be sober today, living in New York, going to college, pursuing a dream if it hadn't been for them?"

Josh scrunched up his face. His indignation still burned, but he turned his gaze inward to see its source. "I don't know," he said.

"Would you have ever become such good friends with Matt if it hadn't been for those trips?"

Josh cocked his head to the side. The ambiguity was hard to hold. "Probably not," he said.

"And if you hadn't learned how to surf, would you have even stayed sober in high school?"

Josh frowned. "I really don't know," he said. "Probably not."

"Well, don't be so quick to judge then," Melody said. "That's always been your problem, Josh. Everything's so all or nothing."

Josh wasn't sure if Melody was still talking about Denny and Laurie anymore. But he didn't want to ask her. He shrugged. "It was also them who sent my mom that video of Bill having an affair," he said.

Melody appeared stunned. "How'd you find that out?" she asked.

"Pete helped Denny mail it."

"And he never told you?"

Josh shook his head. "Not until years later. Some friend, huh? I mean, that video, you know, it might have split up my mom and Bill, but it messed with my mom big time too."

"I remember," Melody said. "Why'd they do it?"

"They were trying to get control of Bill's company. Splitting him and my mom up was just part of the plan."

"Did it work?"

"I don't know," Josh said. He started staring off into space once again. "I haven't spoken with Bill in years either. He lives in New York now though. My mom told me that."

"Do you ever wonder what you'd do if you ran into him there?" Melody asked.

Josh chuckled. "Probably just keep on walking," he said. "That man isn't even worth my time of day."

Melody nodded. "Speaking of bumping into people," she said. "I bumped into Tracy Allen a few months ago. Do you remember her from middle school?"

"Vaguely," Josh said.

"Well she remembers you," Melody said. She laughed. "In fact, she was the mystery girl in the front seat of Ben's car that night you got beaten up by the preacher."

Josh furrowed his brow. He remembered that night, the night of his last drink. He remembered the preacher, the shotgun, and a vengeful girl's gaze in the front seat of Ben's Pontiac Phoenix.

"But there was no preacher," Melody said. She laughed. "You were never even at a church."

This time, it was Josh's turn to appear stunned. He'd told that story a million times over the years—how he'd tried breaking into a church to be saved and how a preacher had come out with a shotgun and instead of helping him had beaten him to a pulp. It was part of Josh's overall condemnation of organized religion. How it never tried to help people. It was only interested in saving itself.

Melody kept on talking, "You were in Todd's apartment complex that night. That was just some random guy whose door you were banging on. If I'd been at my mom's that night, I might have heard you too. I lived there back then too if you remember."

"Wow," Josh said. "I had no idea." He sat up straighter. "I sure am lucky he didn't shoot me."

Melody laughed again. "So am I," she said. She rocked over in Josh's direction and bumped her shoulder against his.

Josh looked down at her. He swallowed slowly. "Melody," he asked, "how come we never dated?"

Melody stopped rocking back and forth. A distant look came into her eyes. She scrunched them up. "I don't know," she said. "We just didn't."

Josh nodded. "I know that," he said. He swallowed slowly. "You knew I was in love with you though right?" Josh paused. He couldn't believe he'd phrased his words that way.

Melody couldn't either. She nodded slowly. "I think I did. I just didn't want to believe it. It would have made everything so complicated."

"But it all got complicated anyway."

"It sure did," Melody said. She looked down. "Once Aaron and I broke up, I used to ask myself that same question—*Why didn't I ever date Josh Marshall?* I never came up with an answer though. It was always just one big question mark." She drew the question mark in the air with her finger. She finished it with a sharp stab at nothing.

Josh nodded. They were silent for a while, breathing in unison together.

Melody asked, "Do you still smoke in here?"

"No," Josh said. "I finally quit. Haven't had a cigarette in almost a year."

"Oh I did too, when I was pregnant," Melody said. "It was just, you know, hanging out with you reminded me of old times." Melody glanced at Josh out of the corner of her eye. "I thought maybe we might share a cigarette again."

Josh nodded. But he wasn't thinking about what Melody was saying right then anymore.

Then Melody said, "We could try it now." Her voice was almost a whisper.

Josh straightened in his seat. He looked over at his friend. She was staring at her feet resting on the ground. "What do you mean?" he asked.

"Dating," Melody said. "We could try it now."

Trying to envision that reality himself, Josh closed his eyes. He didn't see anything. "What would that even look like?" he asked.

"I don't know," Melody said. "We'd have to try it out."

"I live in New York," Josh said.

"Only for the next four years."

"Four years is a long time."

Melody wiped her palms on the legs of her bell bottom jeans. "Not as long as we've known each other already," she said.

Josh tilted his head to the side.

"Come with me," Melody said.

As if awaking from a dream, Josh opened his eyes. He looked at his old best friend. There was a light in her eyes that he'd never noticed before. It was the same as what he'd been trying to fill her with all those years before when he'd laid his hand on her arm in class and tried to pass the golden light he'd inhaled through his nose out through his palms. *"What are you doing, Josh?"* Melody had asked. He'd learned that trick from one of Denny's tapes, but it hadn't worked. Somehow, without doing anything, it worked now.

"I can't leave Noah with his grandma forever," Melody said. "And I want you to meet him." She was smiling. She extended her hand. Josh took it with his own. He was finally aware of the wings that had always graced his back.

Thank You

Just like how there's no such thing as a solitary human being, there's no such thing as a solitary artist. Every person needs others to teach them about themselves. There are so many people in this world who have helped me get to where I needed to get to tell this story today. In particular, however, I'd like to thank my two closest teenage friends—Shannon and Shawn. Without you two, I never would have met Josh Marshall and the other characters who grace the pages of this book. Thank you for all your love and support as we grew and struggled together in our own version of Potterfield County.

I'd also like to thank my fellow authors Kyle Foley and Mel Currie for taking the time to read early drafts of this book and to offer me their invaluable feedback.

And finally, thank you to my wife, PJ, and our amazing children. Without you all, I never would have experienced the life I needed to see this book the way it needed to be seen. I love you all.

Portrait by PJ Adams

About the Author

Michael Anthony Adams, Jr. is originally from Whittier, CA. He holds a master's degree in philosophy from the New School for Social Research in New York City. As a teenager, he was the lead vocalist for Richmond, VA-based hardcore band Broken Chains of Segregation. He's the founder of Ursprung Collective, an international spoken word/music project referred to as "fantastic brain food" on ReverbNation. He was the primary lyricist for Washington, DC-based indie rock band One & the Many's first two albums: *Forms* and *Hours*. His writing has appeared in the *Santa Fe Literary Review*, *The Stray Branch*, *Badlands Literary Journal*, and more. He currently lives with his wife, PJ Adams, and their children in Baltimore, MD.

www.MichaelAnthonyAdamsJr.com

www.ingramcontent.com/pod-product-compliance
Lightning Source LLC
Chambersburg PA
CBHW031438200726
48289CB00002BA/652